MANGO LUCKY

A Walker and Mango Bob Adventure

Bill Myers

www.mangobob.com

Mango Lucky

This book is a work of fiction. Names, characters, places and incidents are either the product of the author's imagination or are used fictionally. Any resemblance to actual persons, living or dead, or to actual events or locales is entirely coincidental.

Version 2012.09.06

ISBN: 978-1-889562-02-5

First Edition: September 2012

1

I never planned to be *that* guy.

You know the one. The guy at the beach with the metal detector. Looking for treasure, but finding mostly bottle caps and pull tabs.

Being that guy was never part of my plan. But it happened. Thanks to Sarah.

See, we were sitting on the boardwalk at Manasota Key beach, late one Wednesday afternoon.

I was watching a group of college girls play volleyball when Sarah said, "You should get one of those."

I nodded, "Yeah, right."

She continued, "I'm not kidding. If you had one of those, you could have a lot of fun."

I was pretty sure Sarah wasn't talking about the college girls so I turned to see where she was looking.

It was an older man with a metal detector.

We'd seen him here on the beach many times before. With his silver hair and sun wrinkled skin, he looked to be about seventy years old.

In his right hand, he carried a metal detector. In his left, a long handled shovel-like scoop.

Around his waist he wore a tool belt, on which he'd hung a white plastic trash bag, a black belly pack, and a dark green canvas bag with 'Garrett' printed on it.

On his head, a tan ball cap with a 'Laurence of Arabia' flap covering the back of his neck. A set of large black headphones covered his ears. A coiled cable ran from the headphones to the metal detector he held in his right hand.

The overall impression was of someone who was serious about what they were doing. Someone who didn't care what others thought about how he looked.

As we watched, the man followed an invisible path along the beach just a few feet above the waterline. He'd take a step, swing his metal detector left to right, then take another step and repeat the process.

His movements were fluid and natural, like that of an athlete who had been training, refining and perfecting the mechanics of the motions for years.

Every few moments he'd stop, swing the detector twice over a spot on the beach, then use his scoop to dig up a bucket of sand.

He'd shake the scoop left to right, sifting out the sand until the only items left were those too big to fall through the round holes in the bottom and sides of the scoop.

Then he'd reach into the scoop, retrieve an object,

look at it closely and either put it in his trash bag or his pants pocket.

After he'd filled the hole he'd dug in the sand, he'd start the process all over again.

Sarah elbowed me, "See, he's finding stuff. You could do that."

I shook my head, "You want me to get a metal detector? And come out here on the beach and spend my days picking up other people's trash? Are you crazy?"

"No, not crazy. Just thinking that since you're the luckiest guy I've ever met, if you had a metal detector you'd probably find treasure in no time."

"Me? Lucky? I don't think so. In the past three months I've lost my job and my house, and my wife divorced me. I'm unemployed, and living in your backyard. That doesn't sound very lucky to me."

Sarah smiled. "Okay, let's review.

"Three months ago when the company you worked for moved their plant to Mexico, you got laid off, but somehow you ended up with a big fat severance check and a free motorhome.

"You drove the motorhome down here to Florida and immediately found a free place to live, close to the beach. My backyard.

"The first day you're here, you buy a lottery ticket, and it turns out to be a winner.

"And then three weeks later, the company that laid you off, pays you a half million dollar whistle blower settlement to keep you quiet.

"So yes, I'd say you were lucky."

I nodded, "OK, I admit buying the winning lottery ticket was pretty lucky. But I gave the ticket to you. So you were the winner. Not me. That makes you the lucky one.

"And the ticket wasn't the grand prize winner. Just sixteen thousand dollars.

"And it was your sister who arranged the motorhome deal. It was part of her secret plan to get me to deliver Mango Bob to you.

"As for living in your backyard for free, you offered that in return for me bringing Mango Bob.

"And finally, the company offered me a settlement just to protect their stock value. I didn't ask for it, didn't even know it was in the works.

"One of their bean counters figured it was good insurance to pay me off instead of taking the chance that I might be required to testified about what I knew."

"So it's not like I'm especially lucky. It's just how things work out sometimes."

Sarah smiled, "Call it what you want. But winning the lottery? Getting a half million dollar payoff? Living free in Florida? I call that lucky."

Rather than argue with Sarah, I kept quiet. It was possible she was right. I did seem to be on a lucky streak lately.

She pointed at the man with the metal detector. "Look, he found something!"

We watched as he bent over and picked up a small object from the sandy beach.

Instead of putting it in his white trash bag as he had done before, he reached into his shirt pocket and pulled out a pair of reading glasses.

Putting the glasses on, he inspected the item carefully. He smiled, then looked around to see if anyone was watching him. Satisfied that he wasn't being observed, he put the object in his shirt pocket.

Sarah elbowed me, "See! He found something good. Maybe a diamond ring!"

I shook my head, "It's probably just a nickle or quarter. Loose change on the beach."

Shaking her head, Sarah said, "I think you're wrong. I've been watching him and he puts different things in different pockets.

"When he finds a bottle cap or pull tab, he puts it in the trash bag around his waist. When he finds a coin, he puts it in his pants pocket.

"This is the first time I've seen him put anything in his shirt pocket, so it must be something good."

Sarah stood, "Let's go talk to him."

2

Sarah brushed the sand from her shorts and headed toward the man with the detector. I followed, catching up with her quickly.

"Sarah, slow down. We don't want to scare the guy off."

She stopped, and gave me the look. The one that says, "You're not the boss of me."

Then she turned and began walking more slowly in the man's general direction. Maybe she decided I was right. No need to scare him off by running up to him.

Sarah is my age, mid thirties, and single like me. She's about five foot four, with the slender build of a runner. Her healthy tan gave the impression of someone who spends a lot of time outdoors.

Today she is wearing a white Columbia fishing shirt over a pair khaki shorts, the kind with lots of pockets. This outfit is part of her 'beach casual' look.

Her chestnut brown hair is pulled back into a pony tail. A pair of sunglasses hang on a cord around her neck. Even a stranger could have guessed she lived near the beach.

Sarah operated Dolphin Kayak Tours, and until recently, she'd been spending eight to ten hours a day giving paddling lessons in the waters of Lemon Bay and the Gulf of Mexico.

As the company's owner and only employee, Sarah had been working hard to build her kayak tours into a profitable business. That meant long hours, low pay, and lean living.

Her office was located in the old Mango Street boatyard, just off Dearborn, in Englewood, Florida.

The boatyard had been vacant for years, and Sarah had been able to work out a deal with the owner for low rent, in return for maintaining the property and keeping it from being vandalized.

It wasn't much, a small concrete block building with an office up front and a tiny apartment in the rear, where Sarah lived.

To the left of the building, a wide gated driveway led into a hard-packed dirt parking lot. Surrounded by a tall, weed-choked chain link fence, the lot consisted of a few decrepit old sheds, where the boats were once stored.

It was there, in the old boat yard, that Sarah allowed me to park and live in my motorhome.

While it wasn't paradise, the old boatyard did have the water and power connections I needed for the motorhome. And the overgrown fence surrounding the lot provided privacy and a sense of security.

I offered to pay Sarah rent, but she said no. Instead, she suggested I help her in her business. She said I could help her load and unload the kayaks for each tour she gave. And paddle along with her group and be there if she needed me.

To me, it really wasn't work. It was a chance to be out on the water in Florida. With Sarah. Everyone else had to pay for that experience.

So I couldn't complain.

There were other benefits as well. Working out in the sun and paddling all day over the water had gotten me back in shape. Tan and lean, I now looked like I did when I returned from my first tour of duty in Afghanistan.

Only now I was happier and wearing civilian clothes.

Speaking of clothes, Sarah felt it important we project a professional image while working with her clients, so she picked out the clothes I wore on duty.

That's why today, I too wore a white Columbia fishing shirt over a pair of khaki shorts.

Together we looked like the perfect beach couple. A matched set.

But looks can be deceiving.

Even though we spent almost every waking hour together, our relationship had yet to move beyond a close friendship.

That was part of the agreement we had.

When we'd first met, I was coming out of a bad marriage, and Sarah had just gotten away from a jerk of a boyfriend. Neither of us was interested in jumping into a new relationship.

So it was agreed I would be permitted to park and live in my motorhome in the boatyard, as long as I abided by Sarah's rules.

The rules were simple.

1. I wouldn't bring uninvited guests onto the property.

2. I wouldn't use drugs or drink excessively

3. I wouldn't play loud music

4. And I wouldn't do anything to attract attention to the fact that I was living in a motorhome in the boatyard.

The most important rule was I had to agree that whenever Sarah told me it was time to go, I'd pack up my motorhome and leave, no argument.

So far, the agreement had worked out well.

Especially for Sarah, since she now had me as free labor to help her in her business.

But again, I'm not complaining.

Working with the kayak tours meant I spent a lot of time with Sarah. And the more time I spent with her, the more I hoped our relationship would turn into something more than just friendship.

So far, I hadn't gotten any signal from Sarah that it would.

We were about a hundred feet from the man with the metal detector when I saw them.

Two men, coming down the boardwalk steps onto the beach. They were walking quickly in the same direction we were heading. Toward the man with the metal detector.

Normally I wouldn't have taken noticed of these guys, but they stood out from the rest of the beach crowd. It was the way they were dressed.

Instead of t-shirts and shorts like everyone else, they both were wearing long black pants, black boots, and black long sleeve shirts. And one was carrying what looked like a tire iron in his right hand.

Not what you expect to see on the beach in the sleepy town of Englewood, Florida.

I reached for Sarah and nodded toward the two men, "See those two guys? Something's up. Let's hang back and see what happens."

As we watched, the two men closed in on the man with the metal detector and stood directly in his path.

When he looked up and saw them, he attempted to walk around the pair.

They stepped into his path again, blocking him.

I looked at Sarah, "Stay here, I'm going to get a little closer."

Sarah whispered, "Don't hurt them."

Sarah knew about my days in Afghanistan. And

she'd seen me in action before. She knew I could handle trouble. She knew I could hurt people if necessary.

As I began walking toward the two men, I stopped, bent over and filled my hands with wet sand. Then I continued in their direction, coming up from behind.

As I got closer I could hear the taller one say, "Give us your trinkets old man, or we'll hurt you."

3

The man with the metal detector ignored the threat. He stepped around the men and walked away.

The two men quickly caught up with him, again blocking his way. The taller of the two put his left hand on the man's shirt, in his right he flicked open a six inch knife and said, "Your money. Now!"

The older man calmly set his metal detector down on the sand, picked up his long metal scoop and held it in front of him, as if he were preparing for battle.

"Get out of my way. I don't want trouble."

The men in black laughed. Moving closer, the taller one flashed the knife, "Give us your money, or get cut."

Instead of giving up his money, the detector guy swung his metal scoop at the taller man, narrowly missing his face.

That's when the shorter man, the one holding the tire iron, put one foot behind the old man's leg and pushed him backward, causing him to topple onto the sand.

At that point I was close enough to take action.

From behind, I walked up and dumped a hand full of sand down the back of the shirt of the taller man.

I'd learned this trick early on.

Distracting and confusing an opponent gives you the advantage. And in this case, sand down the back of the shirt was the perfect distraction.

Feeling the wet sand, the taller man slapped his neck with one hand as if trying to swat a bee, and then used his other hand to reach around and feel the small of his back where the sand had accumulated.

The man was now defenseless, with both hands behind his back.

I turned and repeated the move with the shorter man, dumping sand from my other hand down the back of his shirt. He reacted the same way as his partner.

Both hands behind his back, trying to figure out what was going on.

The man with the detector took this opportunity to swing hard with his long handled scoop, catching the short man on the left side of his knee.

I could hear the knee pop when the heavy end of the scoop connected. Screaming, the short man fell to the sand, dropping his tire iron.

I picked it up.

The taller man started to move toward the detector guy who was now trying to get back on his feet. I stepped between them, tapping the attacker on the chest with the tire iron.

"You really don't want to do this. Too many witnesses."

I pointed to the gathering crowd. "Now would be a good time to leave. While you still can."

From the corner of my eye, I saw the metal detector guy raise his right arm. In his hand, a small pistol.

4

The beach is no place for a gun. Especially when there is a crowd of potential witnesses and victims.

Turning to the metal detector guy, I said, "Put the gun away."

I pointed to the two attackers, already leaving the beach. One was limping, the other mumbling obscenities in our direction.

As the crowd of witnesses scattered, Sarah walked up, "You okay?"

"Yep, no problem. Just a misunderstanding."

I turned toward the metal detector guy who was still holding the gun. "Put it away. If the police show up, you don't want to be holding a gun."

He grinned. "I coulda handled those punks by myself. Me and this pistol. If you hadn't showed up, I would have shot 'em both."

I nodded, and he put the gun back into his belly pack.

Extending my hand, I helped him get to his feet, "I'm Walker. This is Sarah."

He smiled, "Glad to meet you. I'm Ralph."

Looking at Ralph, Sarah asked, "You okay?"

He nodded, "I'm fine. Just a little embarrassed that those punks were able to knock me down.

"They think just because I'm old, I'm an easy target.

"But they'd be wrong. This metal scoop is a pretty good weapon, and if that doesn't work, I've got the little pistol in my belly pack."

He took a breath, then continued, "I'd hate to shoot anyone, but I'm not going to let some punk beat me up."

Sarah nodded in agreement, then asked, "Does this happen often?"

Shaking his head, Ralph said, "Not really. Mostly people just ignore me. Or they come up and ask me questions. Want to see what I've found.

"But once in a while, I'll run into trouble. Usually kids trying to impress other kids. Throwing a Frisbee at me. Things like that.

"This is only the second time someone tried to steal from me. And just like the first time, it didn't work out for them."

Sarah nodded, then pointing at the detector, asked, "So Ralph, what kind of things do you find out here on the beach?"

He smiled. Sarah had that effect on men.

5

"What do I find?" replied Ralph. "You'd be amazed.

"I find bracelets, earrings, watches, even cell phones."

He reached into his shirt pocket, "I found this today. It's a gold ring. With a small diamond."

Sarah looked at the ring, "Wow! You found that today?"

Ralph beamed, "Sure did. Right on this beach.

"Now don't get me wrong. I don't find rings like this every day. In fact, I'm lucky if I find just one a week.

"But I usually find something interesting every time I come out here. Mostly coins. Costume jewelry. And lots of toys."

"What do you do with all the things you find?" asked Sarah.

"If I can identify the owner, I try to return the item. But most things I find aren't marked with an owner ID. So if it's something real valuable, I'll let the lifeguard know, and if someone asks about it, I'll give it back to them.

"The rest of the stuff, I keep. When I need money, I sell some of it."

Sarah nodded, then asked, "So Ralph, how you'd get started metal detecting?"

Ralph smiled, "Had to. Doctors orders.

"See, fifteen years ago my wife and I were living in upstate New York. We got tired of the cold winters and decided to head to Florida.

"After looking around, we decided Englewood was the perfect place for us. Affordable, peaceful, and right on the gulf.

"We bought a small house and settled into the retirement lifestyle. Two years later, my wife died, leaving just me and Porky."

"Porky?" asked Sarah.

"Porky is my dog. A Jack Russell terrorist. He's the boss.

"Anyway, after my wife died, my doctor said I needed to get a hobby that involved daily exercise.

"I didn't like golf, so I took up metal detecting. Been doing it every day for the last twelve years. Except when there's a hurricane."

Sarah nodded, "So if you've been out on the beach every day for the past twelve years, you must of found a lot."

Ralph smiled, "Yep. I have buckets full of coins and other stuff I've found. And three display cases full of rings."

Sarah was impressed. "That's amazing!"

Then she pointed at me and said, "I'm trying to get Walker here to take up metal detecting. What would he need to get started?"

Ralph thought for a moment, "He'll need a good metal detector. And a long handled sand scoop.

"And he'll need a lot of patience. Because you don't just come out here for a few minutes and find buried treasure.

"You have to be out here every day and swing the detector for hours, hoping to find just one good thing.

"If you have the right detector and learn how to use it, and spend enough time swinging it, you'll start to find coins, and eventually jewelry. Maybe even some really nice pieces."

Sarah nodded, "What if Walker wants to find real treasure? You know, pirate gold. Where would he do that?"

Ralph shook his head, "You won't find any pirate treasure on this side of Florida. To find that, you'll need to go to the Treasure Coast on the east side of Florida. Near Vero Beach.

"Over there, under the right conditions, you have a pretty good chance of finding Spanish silver and gold coins."

"Treasure coast?" asked Sarah. "Why is it called that?"

"Well," replied Ralph, "Back in 1715, thirteen Spanish ships loaded with gold and silver were heading from South America to Spain, and got caught up in a hurricane just off what is now Vero Beach, Florida.

"Those ships sunk and dumped two hundred tons of freshly minted gold and silver coins just offshore. And ever since, people walking the beaches over there occasionally find silver and gold coins from the ship wrecks. Especially after big storms."

Sarah nodded, then asked, "So if Walker wants to take his motorhome over there and search for treasure, what should he do?"

"That's easy," replied Ralph. "He should wait until he sees a tropical storm heading for that coast, then get a camping spot at Sebastian Inlet State Park.

"From there, he can quickly get to the best treasure beaches right after the storm passes.

"But before he goes, he should look up the 1715 Fleet wreck on the internet. He'll find maps showing where the ships went down, and the best beaches to search."

Ralph smiled, picked up his detector and stuck out his hand. "Walker, thanks for your help with those punks. If I can ever do anything for you, just let me know. You can always find me out here on the beach."

Then he turned to Sarah, "If you guys don't mind, I want to get back to detecting and see if I can find another ring before the sun goes down."

He pulled his headphones over his ears and started moving down the beach, slowly swinging his detector over the sand.

6

Sarah couldn't contain herself. "Walker, you need a metal detector. Then you could be like Ralph, finding diamond rings on the beach.

"You saw the one he found today. It's probably worth a thousand dollars or more. If you had a detector, you could be finding things like that."

"You're right," I said. "That was a nice looking ring. But look at how many hours Ralph spends detecting each day.

"I'm not sure I want to spend my time that way, alone on the beach swinging a metal detector.

"I'd rather be doing something with you."

Sarah turned toward me, a serious look on her face. "Walker, here's the deal. You've got too much time on your hands. I can't be around you all the time. You need to come up with a hobby or something to keep you busy.

"So think about getting a metal detector. And think about going over to the Treasure Coast for a few days, maybe even a week or two.

"And do it sooner than later. Because we need a break from each other."

I wasn't expecting that. I thought Sarah and I mutually enjoyed each others company.

But maybe she was right. We were spending a lot of time together. And maybe she needed some time alone. Maybe even some time with someone that wasn't me.

I wasn't going to argue with her. If she wanted me to go to the other coast and be a treasure hunter for a few days, that's what I'd do.

"Walker, don't take this personal. It's just that until you showed up, I got used to living alone. Not having to entertain anyone. And I liked it that way.

"And while I've really enjoyed our time together, I really miss being by myself. And there's something else.

"I'm worried you might be getting too attached to me. We both just got out of shaky relationships, and I'm not rushing back into another one with you or anyone else.

"I just want to be friends. That's all. And I want the freedom to do things without you. I hope you can understand."

I nodded, not knowing how to reply.

In my mind, I had built us up as a couple with a romantic future. And I'd done that rather quickly, taking it for granted that Sarah felt the same way.

But she was right.

Since arriving in Florida, I'd spent almost all my waking hours with her. She'd been the only person I knew when I arrived here, and I relied on her to be my guide to Florida life.

Instead of reaching out and making new friends, I had followed Sarah around like a little puppy. And now that she'd mentioned it, I realized how I might be smothering her.

So she was right. It would probably be good if we spent some time apart.

"Okay. You're right. I kind of bulldozed my way into your life. I shouldn't have done that.

"Is it time for me to find another place to park my motorhome? You want me to move out of your life?"

"No," she said. "Not yet. Maybe sometime. But not yet."

She continued, "I don't want you to be mad at me. It's just that I need more space. More time to think about what I'm doing, where I'm going."

I nodded, then said, "Okay. Starting tomorrow I'm going to give you more space.

"And for starters, I'm going to get a metal detector and reserve a camping spot on the Treasure Coast.

"But when I find pirate treasure, I'm not going to share it with you."

Sarah laughed, "Deal. If you find pirate treasure, you can keep it. But if you find a diamond ring like the one Ralph found today, I want it. That'll be my reward for getting you involved in your new hobby."

7

That night, back in the motorhome, I got on the internet and ordered the metal detector and sand scoop Ralph had recommended. I paid extra to have them shipped next-day-air so I'd get them before the weekend.

Then I visited the ReserveAmerica web site and booked a camping spot at Sebastian Inlet State Park for seven days, starting next Monday.

According to the web, Sebastian Inlet State Park wasn't near any grocery stores or restaurants, so it was recommended you bring all the food you needed or be prepared to drive fifty miles round trip to stock up.

The park was located across the road from the 1715 Spanish Fleet survivor's camp, and there were more than seventy miles of Treasure Coast beaches nearby to explore.

After confirming my campsite reservation, I searched Google for 'Treasure Coast' and found a map pin-pointing each of the known treasure ship wreck sites. Several were close to where I would be camping.

For future reference, I printed out one of the maps

and bookmarked the web site. Later on, I planned to enter the names and coordinates of the most promising of these treasure beaches into my GPS.

The more research I did, the more it looked like the entire Treasure Coast was littered with wrecks that had spilled gold, silver, and precious cargo along the beaches.

Surely, with all that treasure buried just a few inches under the sand, I'd have no problem finding something valuable.

Especially if I was as lucky as Sarah thought I was.

8

The next morning, I shared my plans with Sarah. I'd bought a metal detector and would be leaving on Monday for a week long treasure hunting trip.

"So," she asked, "you're headed for Vero Beach on Monday are you? Did you check the weather forecast?"

I hadn't.

She smiled, "According to NOAA, there is a pretty good chance of a storm hitting the Treasure Coast on Tuesday. They're predicting forty to fifty mile per hour winds. And a lot of rain.

"Are you sure you still want to go? Being camped near the beach during a tropical storm might not be a good idea."

I shook my head. "Don't worry about me. I've been through some pretty strong storms and I came out okay.

"And actually, the storm is good news. Ralph said the best time to find treasure on the beaches was right after a tropical storm.

"So maybe it's me being lucky again. Going to the

Treasure Coast just when a storm is supposed to hit."

Sarah touched my shoulder, "Walker, promise me you'll be careful. If it starts looking bad, get somewhere safe and forget about treasure hunting."

She was serious.

"Don't worry," I said. "'I'll keep a close eye on weather conditions. If things get bad, I'll find a safe place to ride out the storm."

After that brief discussion, Sarah and I went our separate ways for the rest of the day. She had business in town, and I needed to take the motorhome to get it fueled up and ready for the trip.

When I talk about my motorhome, most people envision one of those bus sized vehicles owned by the rich and famous. And while I'd like to have one of those, mine isn't quite up to that standard.

Mine is smaller. More along the lines of a UPS truck.

It's officially a Class C motorhome. This means the 'home' part is bolted onto a cut-away truck chassis. You've probably seen a lot of these going down the road.

Bigger than a van, smaller than a bus.

Inside, it's like a small house. It's got a real kitchen with a microwave oven, propane cook top, and a residential two door refrigerator/freezer. In the back there's a bathroom with toilet, and a shower I can stand up in without bumping my head.

Next to the bath, there's a private bedroom with a

TV above the bed, a closet for my clothes and a hidden compartment under the bed to store important things.

Up front, it's got leather seats, a recliner, and a decent size flat screen TV. There's also a dinette table with room for six people. And should I have an overnight guest, the dinette folds out into a queen size bed.

So yes, it's pretty nice. And to me, it's home. Or at least has been for the past three months.

It was originally owned by the company I worked for. They bought it so company executives could use it for business travel.

At least that's the excuse the plant manager gave the corporate bean counters when he submitted the purchase order for the motorhome.

In reality, company executives who needed to travel for legitimate business reasons didn't want to drive a motorhome. They wanted to fly on the corporate jet.

So the motorhome mostly sat unused in the parking lot, except when the plant manager needed to get away for a secret rendezvous with his out of town lover. Without his wife finding out about it.

And that's how the motorhome came to be known as the 'Love Bus'.

When the company closed the plant, they discovered the Love Bus still on their books and still in the back parking lot.

They needed to get rid of it quickly, so they offered to sell it to me way below cost. And had I not been living in a tent at the time, I probably wouldn't have been interested.

But the price was right, and with me living in a tent, buying the Love Bus seemed like a good idea. It gave me a real roof over my head, and a way to travel without worrying about finding a place to sleep.

The only real problem with the Love Bus is it hasn't lived up to it's nickname. There's been no loving on the bus. At least for me.

Hopefully, that would change. Maybe after my treasure hunting adventure.

9

After Sarah left that morning, I decided it was a good time to take the Love Bus to the local Walmart Super Center. There I could fill it with gas and stock it up with food for my Treasure Coast trip.

At Walmart, I bought more than a week's worth of frozen foods, bottled water, snacks, and other necessities. Just because I was camping, there was no reason to go hungry. Might as well have plenty of food on board.

Leaving Walmart, I drove back to the boatyard and put away all the supplies I had purchased. Soon after, a UPS truck pulled up and the driver jumped out carrying three packages.

All were for me. One was the metal detector. The second was the sand scoop. And the third was the 'Metal Detecting Florida Beaches,' DVD I'd ordered from Amazon.

Like a kid on Christmas morning, I quickly unboxed and assembled the metal detector. It took only about ten minutes, and the hardest part was installing the eight AA batteries that powered it.

With the detector ready to go, I went outside, turned it on and started swinging it over the dirt surface of the boatyard.

Almost immediately, I started finding things. Bits of wire, washers, nuts, and my best find of the day, a broken pocket knife.

Even though this wasn't treasure, it did mean the detector was working properly. And that meant I was ready to find gold on the Treasure Coast.

Just before dark, Sarah got back from town. After unloading a few things into her apartment, she came over to see me in the Love Bus.

"Walker, you hungry?"

"Sure am," I replied. "What do you want to do for dinner?"

She suggested we walk over to the nearby Mango Bistro on Dearborn street.

I agreed. And after locking things up, we walked to dinner.

There wasn't much of a crowd when we got there, and we were seated right away.

I ordered the glazed salmon, and Sarah had the garlic shrimp. Our meal came promptly, and as always the case at the Mango Bistro, both the meal and service were excellent.

During dinner, we discussed my planned trip and the potential weather problems. No mention was made of Sarah needing time alone, nor whether I'd have to find another place to live when I got back.

After our meal, we walked back to her apartment, said good night, and went our separate ways.

10

The next morning, Saturday, I woke up early, thinking about my trip to the Treasure Coast. My big concern was the weather. If it turned bad, I might not be able to get there.

So the first thing I did after getting out of bed was to power up my computer and check the forecast.

It didn't look good.

A massive cold front was pushing down the east coast and was predicted to collide with a warm front pushing up from Cuba.

When the two fronts met, they would produce very high winds, dangerous lightning, torrential rains, and flooding in low lying areas.

The forecast put the worst part of the storm right over the Treasure Coast beaches, centered on top of the Sebastian Inlet State Park, where I would be camping.

So much for being lucky.

While the pending storm really didn't worry me, the high winds would make my drive across the state in the Love Bus pretty risky.

One of the down sides of owning a motorhome is they just don't handle well in high winds. The high profile and slab sides create a lot of area for the wind to push around.   Strong, gusting winds, can make it hard to keep them on the road.

 Especially if the roads are flooded.

The possibility of high winds meant if I waited until Monday to drive across the state, my trip might be a wash out.

A better option would be to leave before the winds picked up. This would give me time to get across the state, set up camp in good weather, and then ride out the storm at the park.

If I did that, I could hit the beach with my metal detector immediately after the storm passed. And according to the experts, that was the best time to find treasure.

In looking at the five day weather forecast, today and tomorrow were the best days for driving.

Since the motorhome was already stocked up and ready to go, there was no reason to wait until Monday to leave. In fact, there was no reason to wait until Sunday.

I could leave today, maybe in an hour or so, and be at the campground late this afternoon.

It was the logical thing to do. Leave today. Avoid the possibility of high winds while driving across the state.

With the decision made, I called the campground office and updated my reservation. They said, 'no problem, plenty of vacancies'.

After confirming my reservation, there were only four things I needed to do before I could hit the road.

1. Close the slide room

2. Lower the TV antenna

3. Unhook from shore power

4. Tell Sarah.

These things would only take a few minutes to accomplish. I was outside disconnecting from shore power when Sarah walked up.

"What are you doing?" she asked.

"Getting ready for my trip," I replied.

"I thought you weren't leaving until Monday."

"That was the original plan. But I've decided to leave today."

"You trying to get out before the storm?"

"Yep. I figured I'd leave today while the weather was still nice. Get there before the storm."

Sarah nodded, "That's probably a good idea.

"So how soon you leaving?"

"Pretty soon. Within the hour".

"That fast? You know there's no reason for you to rush off. It won't hurt if you stay here until tomorrow."

I shook my head, "No, there's no reason not to go today.

Then I said, "Of course, you're welcome to join me if you like."

Sarah frowned, "I can't leave. I've got things I've got to take care of next week.

"But you could do me a big favor. You could take Mango Bob with you."

11

"You want me to take Mango Bob? Why would you want me to do that?"

Sarah hesitated, then said, "After you told me you'd be gone next week, I made plans. And Bob might get in the way of those plans.

"So I was hoping maybe you could take him with you."

Mango Bob was Sarah's cat. He and I had spent four days and twelve hundred miles together traveling in the Love Bus on our way to Florida from Sarah's sister's home up north.

As far as cats go, Mango Bob wasn't bad. A 16-pound orange tabby with a two-inch long tail, he was a good listener, knew where his litter box was, and was very good about using it.

He had been no problem on the previous trip and I didn't expect problems from him on this one.

"Sure, I'll be happy to take Bob. But I'm leaving within the hour, so you'll need to get his gear over here pronto so I can get on the road."

Sarah smiled, "Thank you, thank you, thank you. I really appreciate this."

She gave me a hug, then went back to her apartment to get Bob's things.

A few moments later she returned with his litter box and food. I took both inside to the bathroom where Bob expected to find them, placing the litter box in the shower stall, and his food and water bowls in front of the sink.

Outside, I could hear Sarah walking up with Bob cradled in her arms. He didn't seem too happy to have been woken from his morning nap.

Sarah brought Bob up into the Love Bus, and I quickly closed the door behind her. Bob's not normally a runner, but I didn't want to take any chances this close to leaving.

As soon as she set him on the floor, Bob headed to his favorite spot in the Love Bus. My bed.

With Bob settled in, Sarah said her goodbyes and headed out the door.

I did a quick walk around to make sure everything inside was securely stowed. Then I started the motorhome and left the boatyard and Sarah behind.

It was good to be back on the road again.

12

We saw our first alligator thirty minutes into the trip. By 'we', I mean Bob and me.

At first, Bob stayed in the back as I navigated the very busy I-75, but shortly after exiting onto county road 72, Bob strolled up front and hopped up onto the passenger seat. He's tall enough he can see out the side window while sitting up.

Soon after, I spotted the first gator. A six footer that from a distance looked like a rubber retread thrown off a truck tire.

As we got closer, I could see that this retread had four stubby legs, a long tail and lots of teeth. Sunning itself on the side of the road, it was not the least bit bothered by our passing.

I pointed it out to Bob.

"Bob, there's a gator."

He didn't seem to care.

Over the next thirty miles we saw more gators. Mostly smaller ones in the water filled ditches along the road. Also a few larger ones in the creek beds and under the bridges.

I pointed each of these out to Bob.

"Bob, see that gator down there?"

"Bob, there's another one. See it over there?"

"Bob, look at that one, it must be at least ten feet long!"

By this time, Bob was curled up on the seat, purring softly as the sun warmed his body. Occasionally, he would blink a few times at me, but mostly, he just purred.

Nevertheless, I continued to alert Bob of gator sightings.

"Bob, there's a big one down there."

"Look Bob, another one."

After a while I gave up pointing out the gators to Bob. He just didn't care.

Finally, I said, "Bob, I sure wouldn't want to hitch hike along this road, especially at night."

This time Bob answered. "Muuurrff."

I'm not sure whether he was agreeing with me, or asking me to keep quiet so he could sleep.

Fortunately for him, we soon left the alligator area around the Myakka river, and followed county road 72 into Arcadia. From there we got onto county road 70, which took us by the two large state prisons in Desoto County.

No alligators on this part of the trip, but every few miles we'd see a large black animal carcass on the side of the road - a wild hogs that had encountered a car or one of the large trucks carrying oranges from the numerous groves we passed.

Three hours into the trip, we drove through the small town of Lake Placid and continued on around the northern tip of Lake Okeechobee. This part of the state was mostly rural, cattle ranches and grass farms, separated by tropical forests.

It was a pleasant drive. Not much traffic, and a lot of interesting scenery.

Four hours into the trip, we reached Fort Pierce on the east coast of Florida, the first major city we'd encountered since leaving Sarasota on the west coast.

At Fort Pierce, we crossed under I-95 and followed Kings Highway north to US 1, until we reached the small city of Vero Beach. In Vero, we got onto US 60, which would take us to Hutchinson Island - the long barrier island that is the Treasure Coast.

According to my GPS, we were about two miles from the Merrill Barber bridge that would take us off the mainland and onto Hutchinson Island, when we saw a large flashing road sign warning of possible bridge closings due to high winds.

I mentioned this to Bob, who was still sleeping in the passenger seat. "Bob, they say the bridge might close when the storm hits.

"If that happens, we could get stuck on the island with no way off for a few days. Think I should stop and get you some extra food?"

Bob said, "Muuurrph!"

Apparently, he thought stopping was a good idea.

Even though I had plenty of food in the Love Bus, stopping one more time before we left the mainland would give me a chance to stretch my legs, while picking up a few 'just in case' supplies.

As luck would have it, on my right at the next stop light there was a shopping center with a large Publix grocery store, so I pulled in and parked.

"Bob, you're in charge until I get back. Make sure no one gets in."

He yawned, showing all his teeth, and replied, "Murrrph." He had everything under control.

The weather in Florida this time of the year was cool with almost no humidity. And even with the windows closed, the inside of the motorhome would stay well within Bob's comfort zone.

Inside Publix, I picked up a bag of roasted chicken kitty food, Bob's favorite. And for me, I got a few more frozen dinners, another dozen eggs, some bacon, another quart of orange juice, and another case of bottled water.

I didn't need any of this, but there was no reason not to stock up. I had plenty of room and knew from experience that having too much food was always better than running out.

After returning to the Love Bus and securely stowing the extra supplies, we got back onto US 1, and crossed over the bridge onto Hutchinson Island.

Being a barrier island, with the vast Atlantic Ocean to the east and the Indian river to the west, island residents were very aware of the potential damage from even minor storms.

Strong winds could knock out power, tropical rains could quickly produce flooding, and high waves could inundate the streets.

Coming off the bridge, it was clear the locals were taking the coming storm seriously. Retailers were stacking sandbags in front of their stores, others were bolting hurricane panels over plate glass windows.

City maintenance crews were clearing culverts and removing vegetation from storm drains. Dump trucks and backhoes were parked at strategic locations, ready to be used to clean debris after the storm.

It was interesting to see these precautions being taken, even if it seemed like a bit of over-kill.

Sure, a storm was in the forecast, but it wasn't like it was going to be hurricane. Just a day of rain, wind, maybe some thunder and lightning.

Of course, I'd never been on this coast during a winter storm. So maybe the locals knew more than I did about what to expect and how to prepare.

As it turned out, they did.

13

After arriving on Hutchinson Island, I followed the A1A highway toward Sebastian Inlet State Park.

Traffic going north toward the park was light. But south bound traffic coming away from the park heading toward the bridge and off the island was heavy. A steady stream of motorhomes, camping trailers, and trucks pulling boats.

After twenty minutes on A1A, I reached the park, and pulled up to the ranger check-in station. A sign on the window read, "Due to the potential for inclement weather, park services may be curtailed."

Walking inside, a ranger greeted me, "Welcome to to the park. Checking in, or checking out?"

"Checking in. Got reservations for tonight through next Saturday. Name is Walker."

The ranger typed on his computer, "Here you are. You've got a mangrove site in the back. But today is your lucky day.

"There's been a number of cancellations and if you want, we can put you on a river-front site for the entire week."

I nodded, "Sounds good. But is there any risk to being so close to the river? With the storm coming?"

The ranger shook his head, "Not really. If we get a lot of rain, the river will rise a bit. But your campsite is at least eight feet above it.

"And we always keep and eye on things, so if an evacuation becomes necessary we'll let you know."

"Evacuation? You think it'll get that bad?"

"You never know. The weather forecast says lots of wind, heavy rain. Higher than normal tides. Probably some beach erosion. Definitely bad weather for boating."

I nodded, "How about metal detecting? I want to find treasure on the beach."

The ranger laughed. "Yeah, we'd all like to find treasure on the beach.

"Seriously though, you don't want to be on the beach when the storm moves through. But the day after, that's when your chances of finding treasure go up.

"The rules say you can detect from the low water mark to the heel of the dunes. Just don't disturb the sea oats or any vegetation."

After the ranger handed me a camper's check-in package along with a bright yellow card to hang on my rear view mirror, he said, "If the wind really gets going, we might lose power here in the campground.

"It probably won't come to that, but if you see a big storm, you might want to unplug from shore power to avoid electrical spikes."

I thanked him and headed back to the Love Bus.

It was time to set up camp.

14

Driving through the campground, it was easy to see why the rangers had been able to move me to a prime camping spot.

Not many campsites were occupied, and the few that were had people packing up and getting ready to leave.

I shook my head, thinking, "All these people who are leaving are going to miss out on easy pickings on the treasure beaches after the storm."

Finding my assigned camp site, I backed the Love Bus in, and went through the steps of setting up camp.

After extending the slide room, I went outside and connected to shore power and campground water. This would give me all the comforts of home. Free electricity and plenty of water pressure.

Back inside, I opened the coach windows and made sure all the screens were in position. The screens would keep Bob in and the bugs out.

As expected, as soon as the windows were opened, Bob found his favorite perch on top of the couch. From there he could lay against the window screen and feel like he was outdoors.

Our campsite was surrounded by small trees, and the birds that fluttered in and out of the branches captured Bob's attention right away.

He looked up at me, purred a bit, then said, "Murrrph." He was a happy camper.

Since it was late in the afternoon, with only another hour of daylight left, I decided that instead of hitting the beach with my metal detector, I'd just take a walk around the park and get familiar with the layout.

Satisfied that Bob was occupied, I put on my ball cap, grabbed my camera, and slipped out the side door.

Having checked the park brochure, I knew the campground was on a very narrow strip of land, surrounded by water on three sides.

The Indian River to the west, the wide expanse of the Atlantic ocean to the east, and the Sebastian Inlet to the north.

It was a perfect location for a campsite - as long as the weather was good.

In bad weather, there was a good chance there'd be no escape off the island. Something I would discover before the week was over.

15

According to the campground map, a fishing pier on the east side of the park extended three hundred and sixty feet out over the Atlantic ocean.

The pier ran parallel to the Sebastian Inlet, the body of water which connected the Atlantic to the Indian River. The tidal flows of the Atlantic would bring large fish though the inlet and near the pier.

The prospect of catching ocean going fish from the pier was one of the reasons Sebastian Inlet State Park was so popular with tourists and locals alike.

To me, the pier sounded like a good place to get my first look at the Treasure Coast beaches. I figured I could walk out to the end of the pier, and have a long view of the beaches on either side.

It took about ten minutes of walking to reach the pier from my campsite. Normally, at this time of the year, the parking lot by the pier as well as the pier itself would be crowded with tourists and fishermen.

But not today. The parking lot was deserted. Just one older pickup truck. And on the pier itself there was only one person. An older black man with three fishing lines in the water.

As I made my way down the wooden deck of the pier, the lone fisherman turned in my direction and said, "I hope you're bringing me some luck, because I sure could use some today!"

I nodded and pointed to his rod, "I don't know about bringing you luck, but it looks like you got a fish on your line."

He turned, saw the tug on his line and said, "You're right! First bite I've had all afternoon. Let's see what we've got."

He grabbed the rod and began reeling in his line. Slowly at first, then picking up speed as the fish fought to get free. After about three minutes, the fisherman finally brought his catch to the surface.

"It's a snook," he said. "and a good fighter! Look at the size of this one!"

I checked the fish out. It was about thirty inches long, silver in color with a black stripe running the full length of it's body.

The fisherman expertly removed the hook from its mouth and held it up toward me, "You want it? It's good eating."

I shook my head, "Thanks, but no thanks. I've got food back at my campsite."

"If you're sure . . .", said the man. "But if you don't want it, I'm going to put it back in the water."

"Aren't you going to keep it?" I asked.

"No, I mostly fish for the fun of it. So if I'm not going to eat it, I put it back in the water. That way there'll always be something to catch when I come back."

I nodded and started to walk away.

"Hey, don't be in such a hurry to leave. You brought me good luck. As soon as you walked up, I catch a fish. Stay and maybe your luck will wear off on me."

I smiled, "You don't need my luck. You'll do fine without me."

Pointing toward the end of the pier, I said, "I'm going out to end. Check to see what the beaches look like."

The fisherman nodded. "Be careful. That end gets pretty slippery."

I smiled, "Thanks for the warning. Good luck with the fish."

Walking further out, I could feel the pier shudder as large waves from the Atlantic ocean crashed into the pilings below. It was a strange feeling. Not unlike that of a earthquake where the ground below you moves as you struggle to maintain your footing.

The strong wind off the Atlantic blew white caps off the very tops of the incoming waves, leaving tendrils of yellow sea foam on the wooden deck of the pier. This, combined with the constant mist caused by the crashing waves below, created a very slick surface.

It was like walking on black ice. One misstep and you'd be on your butt. I discovered this the hard way.

After almost slipping, I moved close to the hand rail and held it as I continued on, determined to make it out to the very end without sliding off into the crashing waves below.

The thunder of the crashing surf, the wind fighting to knock me down, the rumbling and slippery deck combined to create an air of extreme danger.

It was invigorating.

In the brief ten minutes since I'd left my campsite, the weather had changed. What had started out a clear sky day with a light breeze, had turned to gray overcast skies with chilly gusting winds.

A particularly strong wind gust pushed me across the slippery deck into the railings on the far side. Holding on, I looked down and could see the angry waves crashing into the rocks below.

If I were to fall off the pier into the water, there'd be little chance of survival.

Having had my adrenalin fix, I headed back toward shore.

As I passed the lone fisherman, he said, "My luck went away with you. No bites. No fish."

I smiled, "Maybe the fish heard the weather guys on the radio. Maybe they headed up river to avoid the storm."

The guy just laughed, "Fish don't have no radios."

I laughed in return, and walked back to the motorhome. It was starting to get dark, and I wanted to get settled in for the night.

Before the big storm hit.

16

That evening, I cooked dinner in the microwave and watched the weather report on local TV.

The meal was good. The weather report wasn't.

The storm had intensified, and now they were predicting it would reach the island late tomorrow, and bring with it forty to seventy mile per hour winds. And a lot of rain.

The weather service had issued a series of warnings, including a high surf advisory, a rip tide advisory, a storm surge and coastal flooding advisory, and a small craft warning.

The only good news was the storm was moving fast and should be out of the area in a day or two.

I mentioned the coming bad weather to Bob, and he just said, "Murrph." Translation: make sure I have plenty of food and don't get wet, and I'll be okay.

Since Bob wasn't worried, I wasn't either.

And even if I was, I wasn't leaving the campground any time soon. The wind gusts had made it too dangerous to drive the motorhome. Especially over the bridge that led back to the mainland.

Since I wasn't going anywhere, I decided to make the most of it. I went back to the bedroom, turned on the TV, and popped in the metal detecting DVD I had ordered before leaving Sarah's place.

With Bob beside me, I watched the DVD and learned that I had chosen the right detector and scoop, and would soon be at the right beach at the right time to find treasure.

The expert on the DVD showed me everything I needed to know about metal detecting. How to swing the detector, how to use the scoop, which parts of the beach to detect and which to avoid. He even showed several Treasure Coast beaches, and pointed out hot spots on each.

He also showed some of the treasures he'd found. Rings and coins and gold and silver. The kinds of things I hoped to be finding after the storm.

After the DVD ended, I turned off the TV and checked my phone for messages.

Nothing from Sarah.

I was tempted to call and let her know we had arrived at the campground safely. But decided it was best to give her the space she had requested.

As I was laying in bed thinking about Sarah, the motorhome suddenly rocked from side to side. Bob's ears pricked up and he swiveled his head back and forth, listening for clues. Then he jumped off the bed and disappeared into the open closet.

I got up and went to the front of the coach. The windows were still open from earlier in the day, and a strong breeze was blowing the curtains, causing them to knock against the window frame.

I closed all the windows, pulled the blinds and locked the doors.

In the back bedroom I said, "It's going to be an interesting night, Bob."

He didn't reply. Bob didn't like storms.

17

It was Bob's fault that I didn't sleep well that night. He woke me up with his howling. Three different times.

Each time, he'd start out with a soft meow. Then he would ramp it up, using his outside voice. The more I ignored him, the louder he'd get.

I finally gave in, got up and checked his food. His bowl was full. All he really wanted was reassurance that he wasn't alone.

After a few minutes of talking to him and rubbing his ears, he'd calm down enough to eat a few bites of food and go back to sleep.

It was after Bob's third howling episode that I remembered how I'd settled him down on our previous trip. With catnip.

Looking through the bathroom shelves, I was relieved to find a small bag of catnip, still there from our first trip together.

I crushed up a small amount and placed it on a paper plate in front of Bob. Then I rubbed a bit of it on his face, just behind his whiskers.

Bob said, "Mrrrruuff." He started purring, then walked over to the paper plate, and ate all the catnip I had prepared for him.

A few moments later, Bob was sound asleep.

He slept the rest of night without any further howling episodes.

Catnip, the wonder drug.

The next morning, I woke early. Bob was asleep on the bed. Down by my feet. Snoring contently.

And even though I hadn't slept well, I was ready to get out on the beach with my detector and start finding treasure.

At the very earliest, the storm wasn't scheduled to hit until late this afternoon. I figured I could get in a few hours with the detector before I'd have to come back.

I nudged Bob out of the way, got up, ate a quick breakfast, and suited up for my first real treasure hunt.

18

Before leaving the motorhome, I checked Bob's supplies. Wouldn't be good to leave him alone without food, water and a clean box.

After making sure Bob was set, I headed toward the beach, with detector and scoop in hand.

The campground was quiet except for a few early risers who were packing and getting ready to leave. The few campers left seemed to be in a real hurry to get away.

About half way to the beach I realized I hadn't checked the latest weather forecast. And I'd left my phone back in the motorhome. So no way to check until I got back.

No problem. The sun was shining, the sky was blue, and other than the hint of cold in the steady northerly breeze, there was no indication that a major storm was on the way.

I continued to the beach, confident that not only would I be safe, I'd probably find some treasure before the storm hit.

As it turned out, I was wrong on both counts.

19

When I reached the beach, the sun was still shining, and a cool breeze blew from the north. The waves rolling in from the Atlantic were starting to show white caps, hinting at what was to come.

Since the north side of the beach was blocked by the fast moving waters through the Sebastian Inlet, my only option was to head south.

I powered up the detector, pulled the headphones over my ears, and began my first treasure hunt.

Following the instructions I'd seen on the video the night before, I slowly swung the detector over the sand, listening for the tones that would indicate treasure.

I truly expected to start finding things right away. So I was somewhat disappointed that after thirty minutes, I had found nothing. Not even a bottle cap.

Fearing the detector wasn't working properly, I pulled a coin from my pocket, dropped it on the beach, and kicked sand over it with the toe of my sneaker. Then I swung the detector coil over it.

The detector immediately beeped. The LCD display

indicated a coin, one inch deep.

So the detector was working as it should. That meant there was no treasure on this part of the beach. Not much trash either.

But I wasn't discouraged. Instead of staying on the non productive track I had been following, I moved up half way between the water line and the sand dunes. Then I continued my slow walk to the south, swinging the detector in search of treasure.

After not hearing a sound from the detector for almost an hour, I was startled when it finally beeped loudly. It meant I had found something.

I stopped and swung the detector over the area that produced the beep. It beeped again, confirming that something was there, buried in the sand.

I was hoping it would be a gold coin or perhaps a diamond necklace.

I positioned the pointed edge of the sand scoop over the target location, pushed the scoop bucket down with my foot, and removed six inches of sand.

Shaking the scoop left to right, I let the sand sift out through the small holes in it, until I heard the distinct rattle of metal in the bottom of the scoop.

That would be my treasure.

Bringing the scoop closer, I looked to see what I had found.

It wasn't treasure. It was a fishing leader line with six lead weights on it.

Not gold. Not silver. Not diamonds.

I was disappointed. No treasure.

But on the bright side, I had found something. And that proved that the detector was working.

I put the leader line in the plastic trash bag I was carrying, stretched my arms, then picked up the detector and continued my search down the beach.

Over the next hour, my detecting skills got better and I found several objects. Almost all were fishing related. Hooks, lead weights, and a large fishing lure.

I was happy to be finding things, but still hadn't found the treasure I was looking for.

As I detected, I kept my eyes focused on the sand directly below the detector. And that turned out to be a mistake.

I should have been checking the sky back behind me.

I realized this when I finally stopped for a water break. Turning back toward the pier, I could see angry looking dark clouds rolling my way. The north wind had turned colder and was picking up strength.

I'd been walking south on the beach for more than three hours. And during that time, I'd probably covered three miles or more.

With the low storm clouds on the horizon, it was time for me to head back to the safety of the Love Bus.

If I metal detected all the way back to the pier, it'd take roughly the same amount of time it took me to get to this far - about three hours. And then another fifteen minutes to get back to my camp site.

Based on how fast the storm front looked to be moving, I didn't think I'd have three hours. I might not even have one hour.

20

As I started back toward the campground, I could see that the storm was approaching even faster than I thought. The dark cloud bank, rising high into the sky, was moving quickly.

Far up the beach, I could see a heavy mist, perhaps rain. This meant I was likely to get wet before the day was over.

Rather than waste time, I turned off the detector, pulled off the headphones, and started walking as fast as I could through the soft sand.

With each step, I kicked up a rooster tail of sand, much of it filling my shoes. Every few minutes, I had to stop to dump the sand out.

Soon this wouldn't be a problem. The rain in the distance, along with the incoming tide, would turn the soft sand into a wet slurry. And with each step, the heavy wet sand would stick to my shoes like mud.

The rain came on me suddenly and with an unexpected intensity. Driven by the wind, and cooled by the high clouds, the drops felt like pins and needles on my bare arms and legs.

I was soon soaked to the bone. And the rain didn't let up.

As I slogged onward, the rumbles of thunder got louder, and the flashes of lightning became more frequent. As the storm intensified, I could feel an electrical charge building up in the atmosphere.

The rain and thunder didn't worry me. I'd been out in in worse conditions many times before. But the lightning was a real concern.

Being the tallest thing on the beach, and carrying a metal detector and a four foot metal scoop, I had become a walking lightning rod.

I knew I needed to get off the beach as quickly as possible, but I also knew the only way off was the way I had come.

There were no structures on this stretch of the beach, no houses or shelter of any kind to get under. Just the sandy beach in front of me, the Atlantic ocean to my right, and mangrove swamps over the dunes to my left.

My only option was to continue north toward the fishing pier. And into the rapidly advancing storm.

To reduce my lightning profile, I hunkered over, moved closer to the dunes, and drug the metal scoop on the ground behind me.

As I walked, I started thinking what it would have been like to be one of those survivors of the Spanish fleet caught up in the hurricane of 1715.

They washed up on this same beach. And under similar conditions. Driving rain, heavy wind, thunder and lightning.

But it would have been much worse for them. They were in an unknown environment, exhausted and banged up from fighting hurricane enraged seas. Dumped on a desolate section of beach with no chance of rescue.

They had no food, no fresh water, no marked trails to follow, no protection from the elements.

In comparison, I had it good.

All I needed to do was to continue walking north, and I'd eventually reach the end of the beach, and from there it would be just a short walk to my campsite where I had dry clothes, plenty of food, and a shelter from any storm.

I trudged onward, feeling slightly better about my situation.

The rain continued to come down hard, the wind blew stronger, and I got wetter and wetter.

I'd given up any attempt to clean the sand off my shoes. It was a losing battle. So with each step I was carrying what felt like ten pound weights around my ankles.

Finally in the distance, through the rain and mist, I could see the flashing lights on the fishing pier. This meant I was getting closer and closer to my destination.

My spirit buoyed, I picked up my pace and eventually made it to the slippery rocks that marked the edge of the beach and the path leading back to the campground.

The path led me under the north A1A bridge. And that's where I paused to take temporary shelter. Resting for a few minutes, I took the opportunity to clean the sand and mud off my shoes.

Being under the protection of the bridge, I was thinking I could stay here, and wait for a lull in the storm before I ventured back out.

But the storm seemed to be getting stronger. The lightning strikes were coming more frequently. And if the storm continued to increased in intensity, I might get stuck out here through the night. In wet clothes, no food, and a chilling wind. It wasn't something I was looking forward to.

If I continued on though the rain and lightning, I'd soon be back in the warm shelter of my motorhome. And could have a hot meal soon after.

That sounded a lot better than spending the night under the bridge. So it was decided. I was going to move back out into the storm. And get back to the Love Bus.

Leaving the protection of the bridge, I trotted across the now flooded parking lot, and made my way to the road leading to the campground.

I kept my head low, moving as fast as I could.

Just as I reached the center of the road, a huge clap of thunder sounded directly overhead. And almost immediately, I could feel the tingle that signaled an imminent lighting strike.

Looking in front for immediate shelter, I saw nothing. The heavy rain obscured my vision. I was about to turn back for the safety of the bridge, when a loud car horn sounded directly behind me.

I turned to see an older white Toyota Land Cruiser wagon. It pulled up beside me, the passenger window rolled down and the driver yelled, 'Get in!'

now under another two feet of sand."

I nodded. And then started to shiver in my cold wet clothes.

"You need to dry off. You camping here or do you have a car nearby?"

"I'm camping. Staying for a week."

"So am I. Where's your campsite? I'll drop you off."

"First row, overlooking the river."

"I guess that makes us neighbors then. I'm on that row too. "

I nodded. Too cold to respond.

Anna slowly drove into the camping area, the wipers frantically trying to keep up with the rain. As she got close to my site, I pointed, "Over there. In the motorhome. "

She pulled up and said, "You haven't told me your name."

I held out my wet hand, "Walker."

She smiled, "Glad to meet you Walker. Like I said, I'm Anna, And I'm camping over there. In the tent.

She continued, "Tell you what. Before you go back out on the beach, come over and I'll give you some tips on where to find treasure."

I nodded, "I'll do that. And thanks for picking me up. I was drowning out there."

I dug into my pocket for the keys to the motorhome, grabbed my metal detector and then instead of climbing out, I asked, "Are you allergic to cats?"

22

"Allergic to cats? No. Why do you ask?"

"Well I was thinking of asking you over for dinner tonight. But I've got a cat with me. And some people are allergic to cats . . ."

Anna laughed, "Hold on hot shot. You're asking me to dinner?"

"Sure, why not? You just saved my life. And we both have to eat, and I've got plenty of food, and it'll be dryer inside the motorhome than in your tent."

I waited for her reply.

"Anyone else in there with you?"

"No, just me."

"You married?"

I shook my head, "Nope. Single."

"You running from the law?"

"Again, no. None of that. I just thought since you rescued me, it would nice to invite you over for a meal.

"But it's okay if you say no. Me and Bob will just eat alone. Inside, where it's warm and dry."

"Who's Bob?"

"He's the cat. His full name is Mango Bob. And he's quite the character."

Anna smiled, "So let me get this straight. You're a single guy, living in a motorhome with a cat. And I'm not supposed to think that's strange?"

I shivered in my wet clothes and reached for the door. "Anna, I'll be eating dinner around six. You're welcome to join me."

I opened the door, grabbed my things and made a run for the motorhome, the rain coming down hard.

Anna was still sitting in the idling Land Cruiser as I unlocked the motorhome and stepped inside.

23

Coming in from the rain, the first thing I did was pull off my soggy, sand encrusted shoes. No need to track muck throughout the Love Bus.

Next, I stripped off my clothes, left them in a pile at the door, and padded back to the shower. I moved Bob's litter box out of the stall and turned on the hot water heater.

A few minutes later, I climbed into the shower and let the warm water roll down my body.

If you've ever lived an extended period of time without running water or without the availability of a hot shower, you know that hot showers are one of the greatest luxuries in life.

Ask anyone who has gone without, and they'll agree.

I stayed in the shower until the water changed from hot to warm, then climbed out and dried off.

Remembering that I might have company coming over for dinner, I shaved, changed into clean clothes, and tidied up the bathroom.

Still weary from hours of metal detecting, I flopped

"So", said Anna. "You sure look better now than you did earlier."

I smiled, "Yeah, a hot shower, clean clothes and a short nap will do wonders."

She looked around, "This is a pretty nice place. Is it new?"

"No, it's a few years old. It's new to me though. I just got it three months ago. Been traveling in it ever since."

Anna handed me the wine bottle she'd brought in with her, "I didn't know what we were having for dinner. But I had this wine, and thought maybe we could share."

I nodded "Wine sounds good. Have a seat, and I'll get glasses."

Instead of sitting, Anna asked, "Okay if I check out the rest of the place?"

Before I could answer, she walked to the back of the motorhome, checked the bedroom, then peeked into the bathroom.

It looked to me like she was checking to see if anyone else was here. Probably a smart thing to do when visiting a stranger.

Satisfied that we were alone, she returned to the dining area and sat at the table where I had placed two wine glasses.

I opened the wine and poured us each a glass.

Lifted my glass, I said, "To being rescued by a

beautiful woman."

Anna smiled, touched her glass to mine, and took a sip.

Looking around, she said, "So, where's this Bob you mentioned? I didn't see him anywhere."

"Oh, he's hiding in the back, probably under the covers on the bed. He's kind of shy. Not used to seeing many people. He'll come out eventually."

Anna stood, "I'm going to go back and see if I can find him. Make sure he's not some kind of imaginary cat."

"Okay," I said, "but Bob isn't really good with visitors. If you try to pet him he might not like it."

Of course, Bob proved me wrong.

From the back I could hear Anna speaking in a soft voice to Bob. "You sure are a handsome kitty. I bet the girl cats follow you everywhere."

I expected Bob to duck and run, but instead I heard him purring loudly.

A few moments later Anna returned to the table.

"I found Bob. He let me pet him. Even purred a bit. But what's the deal with his tail?"

I laughed, "He was born that way. They tell me he's an America Bob tail. A short stub for a tail is just the way they are."

Anna smiled, "Kind of makes him look like a bobcat." Then she said, "Oh, I get it. Bobcat, as in 'Bob the cat'. Cute."

I agreed, "Yeah."

She took another sip from her glass, then said, "So Walker, you promised me dinner. What's on the menu tonight?"

I smiled. "We have a variety of choices. We could have spinach and goat cheese pizza, or chicken parmesan, or cajun style chicken, or sweet and sour chicken. Your choice."

Anna smiled, "I'm impressed. You can cook."

"No, not really. I can microwave. And I've got a freezer full of frozen dinners. All varieties.

"Tell me what you want, and we'll have a hot meal in about five minutes."

Anna thought for a moment, then said, "Let's have pizza."

"Good choice. The frozen pizzas actually come out pretty good in the microwave."

I went to the fridge and pulled out two organic cheese and spinach individual pizzas, unwrapped them, and put the first in the microwave.

When that pizza was done, I sliced and plated it, then put the second pizza in to cook.

I carried the two plates to the table, put one in front of Anna and said, "Your dinner is served."

She smiled, "This looks pretty good."

We were both hungry, and it didn't take us long to go through the pizza. Fortunately, just about the time we finished the first two slices off, the bell on the microwave dinged, announcing we each had two more slices to eat.

After we'd finished those, Anna said, "That was pretty good. Not at all what I expected from a frozen pizza."

"The secret," I said, "is in choosing the right pizza and not over cooking it. Being single, I've become an expert at this kind of thing."

Anna smiled, "So how come someone as handy in the kitchen as you, is still single?"

I laughed, "Well, I was married. Then one day, the wife decided it was over. She filed for divorce, and I've been single ever since."

"Divorced, huh? A lot of that going around. In fact, I've been down that road myself. What a mess."

I nodded knowingly.

"So Anna, tell me about treasure hunting. Any chance I'm going to find gold on the beach after the storm?"

25

"Yes," replied Anna. "If you're real lucky, and you hit the right beach just after the storm, you just might find some gold. But more likely, you'll find silver.

"And that's not bad. Finding old silver coins is pretty exciting. A lot of them are still out there. And some can be quite valuable.

"And even if you don't find gold or silver, you'll probably find something from the treasure fleet. Old iron nails, copper and brass fittings. Even broken pottery.

"And if you're really lucky, you might even find an emerald."

"An emerald?" I asked. "With a metal detector? How is that possible?"

"Well," she replied, "while the Spanish were mining for gold and silver in South America, they found emeralds. Knowing they were valuable, they put them on the ships to send back to Spain.

"When the ships went down, the emeralds went down with them. They'd get encrusted onto metal objects in the ship's debris field. They'd wash up on the beach, and every once in a while, people would find them. Even with a metal detector."

I nodded, "Cool. So tell me, how long have you been detecting on the Treasure Coast?"

Anna paused, then said, "I've been coming to these beaches for years. Usually on weekends or whenever I could get a few days off from work."

"And I've been pretty lucky. I've found a few old Spanish coins, some jewelry and lots of small iron artifacts.

"But no gold. That's what I really want to find. And I'm thinking this storm might be the lucky break I've been looking for."

I nodded, "So you've found some Spanish coins? What was that like?"

"Pretty exciting. At first I thought they were just iron chips because they were heavily encrusted and so small. But when I got home and looked at them closer, I realized they were Spanish Reales, pieces of eight.

"The small ones I've found really aren't worth a lot, but it's always exciting to find a three hundred year old coin."

Anna took a sip of her wine, then asked, "So what have you been finding with your detector?"

I laughed, "Today was my first day using a metal detector. And after five hours on the beach, all I have to show for it is a few lead fishing weights."

Anna smiled, "At least you found something. Proves

your detector is working the way it should.

"If you hang around until after the storm, you'll do better. Especially if you search the beach I'm going to."

I waited for her to tell me more about her special beach, but when she didn't, I changed the subject, "You mentioned getting days off from work to search the beach. So what kind of work do you do?"

She shook her head, "Until recently I worked for the power company as a meter reader. But now that they've put in smart meters, they don't need people like me to go house to house to read the meters any more. So I'm out of a job.

"But I'm not worried about it. I've got a little money saved up, and a couple of job offers I'm considering.

"What about you Walker? What do you do for a living?"

I smiled, "I guess you could say I took an early retirement.

"See, the company I worked for closed their plant and moved it to Mexico. They laid me off, and I ended up with this motorhome and a little money in the bank. So I decided to come to Florida and just camp out for a while."

Anna nodded, "Sounds like fun."

I agreed. "It has been so far."

I changed the subject again, "So back to metal detecting and finding treasures. You mentioned you might share some tips with me. How about it?"

For the next hour, Anna shared her secrets for finding treasures, along with a list of beaches she planned to hit right after the storm.

Her strategy was to avoid the beaches that everyone else would be detecting, because she felt those beaches would soon be hunted out.

So instead, she was going to a secret beach access point that most people weren't aware of. She'd had luck at this beach before, and felt it was the best place to start after the storm.

After telling me of her plans, she said, "If you want to, you can come with me."

I smiled. "That'd be great. I'd love to detect your secret places with you. But aren't you worried I'll find the treasure that should rightfully be yours?"

She laughed, "If only it were that easy. The beach we are going to detect is about three miles long and a hundred yards wide. No way two people can cover it completely.

"So no, I'm not worried about you finding all the treasure. They'll be plenty for both of us. And anyway, it's a lot safer if there's two of us on the beach together."

Later on, I'd find out she was right.

26

Anna and I continued our conversation late into the evening, not realizing the weather outside was getting worse, until a strong gust of wind rocked the motorhome violently.

"Did you feel that?" Anna asked.

"Yeah, the wind's really picking up. Maybe we should check the TV to see what they're saying about the weather."

I used the remote to power on the TV, and we scanned the channels until we found the local news.

They had a weather warning banner scrolling across the bottom of the screen and the newscaster said the weather report was coming up next.

Anna whispered, "Good timing."

We listened as the weatherman described the storm and displayed maps showing its progress.

According to 'Stan the weather man,' the storm had gathered strength and had also slowed down, meaning it would be churning overhead for at least the next twenty four hours.

27

Anna returned a few minutes later, a gym bag in one hand, a flashlight in the other.

"Hope you don't mind, but I figured I might as well bring some dry clothes with me. Everything in the tent was already starting to get wet, so... "

She set the gym bag down, unzipped it and pulled out a bottle of wine.

"And I thought since we're not going anywhere, maybe we'd drink a bit more wine before we turned in."

I smiled, "Okay, but just one more glass for me. After that, I'm calling it quits."

I went to the kitchen and got a box of crackers, a block of sharp cheddar cheese, a plate and a knife. When I returned to to the table, Anna had already poured us both another glass of wine.

"So Walker, tell me more about yourself. What kind of work do you do? Any kids from your marriage? Girlfriends?"

Shaking my head I said, "After I got out of the military, I got into computer network security. That's what I was doing until recently. But I don't think I'll be doing that any more. I don't like working for big companies and dealing with corporate politics.

"And I don't have any kids. And just the one ex-wife. And when it comes to girlfriends, I'm not sure."

Anna laughed, "You're not sure whether you have a girl friend or not? What's that supposed to mean?"

I paused, then said, "It means the girl I thought I was involved with, recently told me she needed more time alone. And that we could be friends."

Anna shook her head, "So you weren't dating? No kissing, no hooking up?"

"No, nothing like that. I was hoping we were moving in that direction, though."

Anna reached out and patted my hand, "Walker, it doesn't sound good. When a girl tells you she needs more time alone and wants to be friends, it usually doesn't end well."

I nodded, "Yeah, I'm starting to realize that. But I'm not giving up just yet. But enough about me, what about you? Any kids? Boyfriends?"

She shook her head. "No kids. No boyfriend. And no job. Just living the dream here in Florida."

Anna finished her glass of wine and reached for the bottle to pour me another.

Before she could pour, I said, "I've had enough. I'm going to bed."

Putting the bottle back on the table, she said, "Okay,

I've probably had enough, too."

I stood and cleaned off the table where we'd been eating, and showed Anna how to lower the table and arrange the cushions to make it into a queen size bed.

From the overhead compartment, I retrieved sheets, a pillow and a blanket and placed them on the bed cushion.

"Here you go. All the comforts of home."

Anna picked up her gym bag, unzipped it said, "Walker, before you go back to your bedroom, there's something I need to show you."

She reached into her bag and pulled out a black leather holster holding a nickle plated revolver.

28

"You've got a gun."

Anna nodded. "Yes, I do. And I wanted you to know about it. I don't want there to be any surprises or misunderstandings during the night."

She continued, "It's not that I don't trust you. It's just that I almost always carry a gun. And I always sleep with one.

"I didn't want to leave it in the tent or my car tonight, so I brought it here."

She slid the gun back in her gym bag.

I didn't say anything.

"Does it bother you that I have a gun? Would you rather I didn't tell you about it?"

I hesitated, then said, "I can understand why a single girl camping in a tent might want to carry a gun. But do you know how to use it?"

Anna nodded, "Yes, I know how to use it. I've taken the safety course, and even have a concealed carry permit, so I'm perfectly legal."

I sighed, "Well, I'm glad you told me about it. But do me a favor. There's a good chance Bob will try to climb into bed with you tonight. Please don't shoot him.

"In fact, try not shooting anybody in here, okay?"

Anna smiled, "It's a deal. And just so you know, I take carrying a gun very seriously. It's not a toy, and not something to play with.

"I just wanted you to know I had it in here. And if that bothers you, I can go sleep in my car."

I shook my head, "No, it's okay. I appreciate you telling me about it.

"And since you're being honest with me, I might as well tell you I have a gun as well. I don't sleep with it, but I do have one back in the bedroom.

I continued, "So it's settled. We both have guns. We both promise not to shoot each other, and we promise not to shoot Bob."

Anna smiled, "Agreed."

29

"So," I said, "here's the sleeping arrangements. I'll be sleeping in the back, and I'll pull the privacy curtain between my bedroom and the bathroom.

"We have to leave the bathroom door open because that's where Bob's litter box is. You can close the door when you're in there. Just be sure to leave it open when you leave."

Anna nodded and I continued.

"Bob will probably cry at least once during the night. Usually it means he's getting ready to use his box. Just ignore him and he'll quiet down after a few minutes.

"And I may get up during the night to pee. Please don't shoot me when I do."

Anna laughed. "Okay, no shooting in the bathroom."

Smiling, I pointed to the back, "You can find clean towels in the bathroom cabinet.

"If you get up before I do in the morning, feel free to do whatever you do in the mornings. If you get hungry, there's bacon, eggs, and orange juice in the fridge.

"Any questions?"

Anna smiled "I think you covered everything. Except the part about locking the outside doors."

"Thanks for reminding me. I'll do that now. You can double check later if you like."

I checked the doors, then said, "All locked. You'll be safe tonight. No one's getting in."

Pointing to the back, I said, "It's been a long day. I'm going to bed. See you in the morning. "

Anna smiled, "Thanks for letting me sleep over."

In the back, I brushed my teeth, then crawled into my small bed and pulled the privacy curtain.

A few moments later, I heard Anna walk into the bathroom and close the door behind her. Then after a few moments, she opened the bathroom door and went back up front to her bed. She had remembered to leave the door open for Bob. That'd keep him happy for a while.

With the noise of the storm and the excitement of having a stranger sleeping just a few feet away from me, I didn't expect to fall asleep quickly.

But I did. It'd been a long day. I'd drank a bit too much wine, and it finally caught up with me.

I was soon sound asleep.

30

I woke to the smell of bacon. And movement in the coach.

Anna was cooking breakfast.

Pulling on pants and a t-shirt, I rolled out of bed and into the bathroom, where I brushed my teeth and ran a comb through my hair.

Hearing that I was up, Anna called out, "I hope you like microwaved scrambled eggs, because that's what I made. Your plate's ready."

Walking up front, Anna greeted me by pointing to the table and asking. "You want orange juice?"

I nodded.

She continued, "I didn't find any coffee so I'm guessing you don't drink it. Me neither. Never got the habit."

I was smiling at her.

"What are you smiling at?" she asked.

"I'm smiling because I woke up to someone cooking me breakfast. That rarely happens. Especially someone as cute as you."

Anna waved her spatula at me, "Don't get used to it. This is a one time thing. You let me sleep on the couch last night, so as repayment, I cooked your breakfast."

"So, Anna," I asked, "how was it? Sleeping on the couch?"

"Pretty comfy," she said. "A whole lot better than sleeping in the tent or in the back of the Cruiser.

"And I didn't sleep alone. Bob slept with me most of the night."

I chuckled, "Bob slept with you? That makes you pretty special because Bob's careful about who he snuggles up to."

Anna smiled, "That's hard to believe. Because as soon as I turned out the lights he was up on the bed with me. And he was still beside me when I got up this morning.

She then pointed outside, "You'll notice it's still raining pretty hard. And the river's come up quite a bit."

I nodded, "Guess we won't be going out on the beaches today. Maybe we should check the weather."

Picking up the TV remote, I turned to the same local weather channel we had watched the night before.

According to the weather guy, the storm had stalled over Hutchinson Island, just north of Vero Beach and would likely dump another four inches of rain before it moved south later this evening.

The lightning had increased in intensity along with the wind, and residents were being advised to stay indoors. Bridges on the island were still closed due to high winds.

The heavy rain was causing low lying areas to flood, and those in flooded areas were told to seek higher ground.

Anna pointed at the radar image, "Looks like we're pretty close to the eye of the storm. Could get messy out there."

I was just finishing my breakfast when we heard a car pull up outside. A few moments later a knock at the door.

It was one of the park rangers.

"Hate to bother you folks, but the park is closing.

"You can stay here in the campground, but you need to move to higher ground away from the river. Up by the restrooms is the best place."

The ranger wiped rain from his face and continued, "The rising water means we have to turn the power off to all the campsites. No electricity until the waters recede."

"And there's a boil order. If you connect to campground water, you need to boil before drinking it."

"Any questions?"

I shook my head.

"Okay then. Move up to the high ground and you'll probably be safe. Don't drink the water and don't hook up to electricity."

The ranger left.

I turned to Anna, "Looks like we're going to be moving."

31

After the ranger left, we cleaned up our breakfast dishes and I prepared to move the Love Bus to higher ground.

Anna held Bob while I ran the slide room back in. I then pulled on my rain jacket, went outside and disconnected from shore power and water.

Before going back inside, I did a quick walk around to make sure everything was disconnected and ready to go.

It wasn't.

The TV antenna was still up. Didn't want to drive with it that way. It'd be too easy to break it off passing under tree branches.

Back inside, I stripped off the wet rain coat, and cranked down the antenna. The Love Bus was now ready to go.

Anna pointed outside, "My Land Cruiser is in your way. I'll leave first. Give me about ten minutes to find a campsite up there, then you follow."

I nodded, "Be careful."

Anna pulled on her raincoat, grabbed her car keys and headed outside.

I watched as she ran through the rain, unlocked the driver's door and climbed in. The Land Cruiser started without any difficulty and Anna drove off in search of higher ground.

Seeing that she was having no problem with the wet road, I returned my attention to getting ready to move. That's when I noticed she had left her gym bag beside the dinette table. With her gun still in it.

Not wanting to chance it spilling out while I was driving, I picked up the bag and placed it in one of the overhead compartments. Then I moved to the driver's seat, started the motor and drove off in the same direction Anna had.

I knew from the campground map, that the campsites were located around a series of circular drives, and at the center of each circle was a rest room building.

To get from my current campsite, which was on the outer most circle, to the rest room building, I needed to follow the road to the first big curve, and then turn left onto the inner circle road.

Shouldn't be a problem.

It took less than three minutes for me to find the turn to the inner circle leading to higher ground. And soon after, I could see the spot Anna had chosen for us, her white Land Cruiser parked beside it.

She had chosen well. A site adjacent to the

campgrounds restrooms. The concrete block structure would provide some shelter from the howling wind.

I carefully parked in the spot she had selected, making sure to leave room for the slide-out on the driver's side.

As soon as I turned off the motor, Anna tapped on the door, then came it. She stripped off her rain coat, saying, "Man, it's nasty out there. The rain just keeps coming down."

Then she smiled, "So how do you like my campsite choice?"

"You did good," I said. "That building should block a lot of wind."

She nodded, then asked, "Did you notice any other campers? The ranger said there were others, but I didn't see anyone else."

"No," I replied. "I didn't see anyone out there. Maybe we've got the place to ourselves."

She smiled, "So, no electricity. And no water. Does that mean no TV and no microwave dinners?"

I shook my head, "Don't worry. Everything in here can run on battery power. Except the microwave, and for that we can start the generator.

"So we're set. But I'd like to run the slide room out. Would you go back and make sure Bob is out of the way?"

As soon as Anna had located Bob and gave the all clear, I pressed the button to extend the slide room. The floor rumbled as the slide slowly went out, opening up more floor space inside.

With the slide completely out, Anna came to the front and said, "Now that we're both awake and already a little wet, let's go somewhere."

I turned to her, "Are you crazy? You want to go out in this storm?"

She nodded, "Yep, we can take the Land Cruiser. It's got four wheel drive, and we won't have any problem getting around.

"We can go out and do a little reconnaissance. Check out the condition of the beaches and roads.

"And it's not like we've got anything else to do. How about it?"

I really didn't want to go back out into the storm. I'd had my fill of it yesterday. But I didn't want Anna going out without me.

"Are you sure you want to go out in the storm? They said to stay off the roads."

Anna pulled on her rain coat, "I'm going to go check things out. Are you coming?"

Reluctantly, I said, "Yes."

And that was a mistake.

32

"Get your raincoat," Anna said. "You're going to need it."

We were heading out into the storm. I wasn't sure that was such a good idea. I'd rather heed the warnings being repeated every few minutes on local TV. Stay indoors, stay off the roads, don't go out except in emergencies.

But Anna was determined to go, and I wasn't going to let her go alone. So I opened the hatch where I'd stored her gym bag and handed it down to her. Then I pulled on my raincoat, and headed out the door behind her.

The rain was still coming down hard, and the high winds had littered the road with leaves, palm fronds and other assorted debris.

"Are you sure you want to do this?" I asked.

Anna smiled. "It'll be fun. And if it starts to look dangerous, we'll come back."

"It already looks dangerous to me," I muttered.

Anna either didn't hear me or chose to ignore my

comment. Leaving the safety of the Love Bus behind us, Anna put her Land Cruiser into gear, and we headed out.

Getting through the campground was easy. The heavy Land Cruiser with full time four wheel drive and high ground clearance had no problem driving over the downed debris.

Reaching the main gate, a sign had been posted indicating the park was closed. The sign probably wasn't necessary since all the bridges to the island were closed and no new campers would be able to reach the campground.

Leaving the park behind, Anna pulled out onto A1A, the two lane road that runs along the edge of the beach for the full length of Hutchinson Island. We headed south.

A1A, like the road in the campground, was carpeted with palm fronds, leaves and branches blown down by the storm.

Anna drove slowly, dodging the larger piles of debris, her wipers running full speed trying to stay ahead of the pouring rain.

We had gone about three miles when Anna slowed and then stopped.

Up ahead, the road was no longer visible. Instead of pavement, all we could see was water.

Anna pointed to the water, "This is the narrowest part of the island. Only about 500 feet wide.

"The Atlantic is on one side, the Indian River on the

other. And judging by the water on the road, it looks like the Indian River has come up out of its banks.

"That's not good. If it rises up high enough to wash out the dunes, it could cut a new channel to the Atlantic, and that would be real bad.

"It would mean this part of the island would be completely cut off from the mainland until a new bridge was built. That could take years."

Looking into the rear view mirror, she said, "We need to turn around. I'm not going to try to drive through that."

As Anna shifted into reverse, I shouted "Stop!"

She slammed on the brakes. "What!"

I pointed, "Look over there. That car on the side of the road."

Anna looked where I was pointing, and she saw what I saw. A small car sitting on the beach side of the road, water up to its door sills.

She nodded, "Looks like someone pulled off the road and got stuck in the sand. When the water recedes, they'll get a wrecker to pull it out."

"Anna, look closer. There's movement inside the car. Somebody's in there."

Anna wiped the fog from her window, and looked again. "You're right. There's definitely someone in there."

Then she said, "You know we've got to try to rescue them."

I nodded, "You got any rope?"

As it turned out, Anna did have a thirty foot bright yellow tow strap in the back of the Land Cruiser.

She explained it this way, "When you spend enough time on this coast, you learn to be prepared. I always carry a tow strap. Too many tourists park in the sand, and need help getting out."

She pointed to the back, "I'll get the tow strap, and you go talk to the driver. Tell him we'll try to pull him out."

I reluctantly stepped out into the driving rain. The water in the road was almost up to my knees and rising fast. It was cold and murky.

Hunching over to shield my face from the wind and stinging rain, I made my way over to the car.

As I got closer, I could hear barking. A dog. Inside the car.

When I reached the car I was surprised to see that the dog was alone. No one else was in the car.

I double-checked to make sure. I went around to each window and looked in. The dog was alone. No one in the front seat, and no one in the back.

Just a big black dog. Standing in the driver's seat, wagging his tail. Very happy to see me.

No signs of anyone else.

I wondered what kind of person would abandon their car in flood waters, leaving their dog to drown?

I looked at the dog and said, "Don't worry buddy,

we'll get you out."

I tried the driver's side door, but it was locked. All the others were locked as well. All the windows were rolled up.

Turning back toward Anna, I shouted, "No driver. But there's a dog."

My voice was drowned out by the roar of the storm. Anna couldn't hear me.

Wading back through the flood water, I finally reached the Cruiser and Anna. Pointing back behind me, I said, "No one's inside. Just a big black dog. "

Anna thought about it, then said, "Well the dog didn't drive out here by himself. Maybe the driver got out looking for help."

Looking around, we could see the only place the driver could go would be up over the beach dunes toward the Atlantic. And there wouldn't be any help that way.

"What if," suggested Anna, "the driver of the car is out on the beach metal detecting. Maybe he doesn't know the water is up over the road."

I nodded, "That's possible. But no matter what, we can't leave the dog. He'll drown if the water comes up much further. So we either find the owner, or we break into the car and take the dog with us."

Pointing at the sand dune, I said, "I'll climb up there and see if I can see anyone on the beach."

I waded back through the water to the car, then left the road and turned toward the dune. It was thick with sea grapes, but there was a small path leading to the top. I followed it.

As I neared the top of the dune, the wind hit me. Coming straight off the white caps of the Atlantic ocean, it was full of foam and sand.

Shielding my eyes, I scanned the beach, looking for the driver of the car.

It didn't take long to find him. He was about twelve feet below me with a metal detector in one hand and a sand scoop in the other.

He was furiously digging a hole in the sand, which the incoming tide and pouring rain was filling back in almost as fast as he was digging it out.

"Hey!" I shouted and waved my arms overhead, trying to get the man's attention.

No response.

He either didn't hear me or was ignoring me.

Rather than waste time shouting, I made my way down to the base of the dune and stood directly in front of the man.

He looked up, "What the hell? What are you doing here?"

I pointed over my shoulder, "The Indian River is flooding. You car is nearly under water. Your dog is going to drown."

Still digging, he said, "I can't leave now. I finally found it."

I grabbed his shoulders with both hands and shook

him. "You're leaving now. Either on your own, or I'm carrying you out. Nothing you've found here is worth losing your life for."

He looked me in the eye and said, "You have no idea."

Then he shook his head, picked up his detector and said, "You're right. It's not worth dying for. And I can't let Jake drown."

I pointed, "You first." Not trusting that he would follow me.

When we reached the top of the dune, we could see how far the Indian River stretched out in front of us, and how it had flooded the road.

The man said, "Damn. I didn't realized it was rising this fast. I've got to get Jake out of here."

Apparently, Jake was the dog's name.

We climbed down the dune to the car. Jake was barking inside, happy to see his owner return.

At the car, I said, "See if you can drive out. If not, we'll pull you out."

The man nodded, and used his remote to unlock the car. He opened the back door and put his metal detector and sand scoop inside.

He then climbed in the driver's seat and started the motor. Putting the car in gear, he tried to pull forward, but his tires just spun in the sand.

I tapped on his window. "Kill the motor. I'll get the tow strap and we'll try to pull you out."

Back at the Land Cruiser, I filled Anna in on the situation. The guy was metal detecting in the storm. Didn't realize the water had come up. Now his car was stuck and we needed to get him out.

My plan was to connect the tow strap from the Land Cruiser to the car. I'd signal Anna when it was time to pull.

Connecting the strap to the Land Cruiser was easy. It had large tow hooks below the front bumper. Took only a minute to get it done.

Connecting the other end of the strap to the car was much more difficult, as half of the car's front end was under the rising water.

It took me about ten minutes to dig out the sand under the car's bumper and find a place to secure the tow strap.

When it was secure, I tapped on the driver's window and said, "Start your motor, hold your foot on the brake, and put the car in neutral. When you see the tow strap tighten, take your foot off the brake so we can pull you out.

"When you see the Cruiser stop and the tow strap go slack, put your foot on the brakes. Don't hit the Cruiser."

The driver nodded, and I signaled Anna to start pulling.

She put the Cruiser in low four, then in reverse, and began backing up slowly.

The tow strap pulled taut and I signaled the other

driver to get off the brakes. I moved behind his car, just in case the strap broke.

At first, the Cruiser seemed to struggle, all four tires trying to find grip on the wet pavement. Then it dug in, and the car at the other end of the tow strap jolted as its tires broke loose from the sand.

With the car released from the sand's grip, the Cruiser had no problem pulling it through the flood waters and out onto A1A.

Anna continued in reverse, pulling the car to dry pavement just beyond the edge where the Indian River had flooded the road. Seeing the car was high and dry, she coasted to a stop.

I tapped on the now unstuck car's window, "Kill the motor. I'll unhook the tow strap."

Not wanting to be accidentally run over, I waited until the driver put the car in park and turned off the motor before I attempted to disconnect the strap. Then I got down below the car's bumper and got to work.

As I lay on my back on the wet road, trying to untie the knot in the tow strap that had been pulled tight, I noticed the wind was creating small white caps on the flood waters that crossed the road.

This was not turning out to be a good week. I was laying on my back on a wet road. I was soaked to the bone, cold, covered in sand, and for the second day in a row, I was outside in a dangerous storm.

After finally getting the tow strap unhooked, I went

back to the driver and said, "You're set to go. Be careful."

As I was about to walk away, the man behind the wheel said, "Wait. Take this."

He handed me a small coin. My reward.

I shook my head and walked back to Anna in the Cruiser. There, I unhooked the other end of the tow strap, coiled it up, and put it in the back seat.

When I finally climbed into the passenger seat, Anna asked, "So what did he say?"

I shook my head, "Nothing. He just handed me a quarter for our trouble."

While we were still sitting there talking about this, the man in the car waved as he drove by, heading north on A1A.

At least he was smart enough not to try to drive south into flooded road.

33

We were in Anna's Land Cruiser, heading back to the campground. I was soaked from head to toe after spending almost an hour in the pouring rain trying to rescue the man and the dog.

Anna was doing all the talking while I was doing my best not to shiver in my wet clothes, chilled to the bone for the second time in as many days.

"I hope that guy knows how lucky he is. If you hadn't dragged him off the beach, the car would be under water, and his dog would have drowned."

I just nodded.

"Did he even thank you? Nope, he just smiled and drove off."

We turned into the campground, drove around the closed gate, and headed to our campsite.

As soon as Anna parked, I dug the motorhome keys out of my pocket, and climbed out of the Cruiser.

Unlocking the door to the Love Bus, I stepped in, turned to Anna and said, "Shower. You first?"

She smiled, "Shower? That sounds like a great idea.

If you don't mind, I'd be happy to go first."

I nodded, "Okay, but I've got to go back and move Bob's box and turn on the hot water."

While I was in the back, Anna stripped down to her bra and panties, leaving her wet clothes and muddy shoes by the door.

Walking back up front, I nodded appreciatively and smiled big.

She shook her head, "Don't get any ideas."

"Hard not to with you looking like that," I said.

Anna smiled, "Remember, I've got a gun."

I pointed to the back of the Love Bus, "Your shower awaits."

While Anna was in the shower, I stripped off my wet clothes and dropped them in a pile near Anna's.

When I did, the coin given to me by the man we had rescued rolled out of my pants pocket and onto the floor.

I picked the coin up, and saw that it wasn't like any coin I had ever seen before. Instead of being round like a quarter, it was rough edged and multi-sided.

The coin was dark and the face was worn smooth. In the center, a large cross surrounded by patterned lines. Around the edges, roman numerals.

I had a suspicion I was holding one of those Spanish reales I'd seen on the internet. A silver piece of eight from the 1715 Spanish treasure fleet. Or a modern-day replica.

Anna would know for sure.

I wrapped the coin in a paper towel and put it in one of the cup holders near the driver's seat.

34

From the back of the motorhome, Anna called out, "Walker, I need some help back here. I'm all out of dry clothes. You got anything I can wear?"

She was standing outside the bathroom, wrapped in a towel.

I laughed, "You look pretty good with just that towel around you. You could wear that all day if you want."

"Yeah sure, I'll do that. Just let me get my gun."

I laughed, "No need for that. Look in the bedroom closet and you'll find t-shirts and shorts. Take whatever you need."

A few minutes later Anna came to the front wearing one of my t-shirts and a pair of baggy shorts.

"So how do I look?" She asked.

"Very fashionable," I said.

Anna smiled, and for the first time I realized she had sparkling green eyes.

"Walker, what's the funny look on your face?"

"Oh nothing. Just thinking it's time for my shower."

Anna smiled, "May I suggest taking a cold one?"

I laughed, then walked to the back, found some clean clothes, and took a short shower.

When I came back up front, Anna was going through the kitchen cabinets.

"Need any help?" I asked.

"No, just looking for something for lunch. Maybe some of this Cajun Chicken Gumbo soup you've got here."

I nodded, "Yeah, that does sound good. You want me to do it?"

Anna removed the can of soup and a large Pyrex bowl from the cabinet. "No, I think I can handle making soup. You just sit down and relax."

Five minutes later, we were at the dining table eating.

Anna spoke first, "So, after we eat, you'll be ready to go out again, right? Rescue some more people?"

I smiled, "Sure. But this time, I'll stay in the Cruiser, and you can wade through the water and climb the dunes."

She laughed, "Yeah, you kind of got the short end of that deal. Maybe we ought to just stay inside here until the storm clears. "

I nodded, "Sounds good to me."

After we finished our meal, I put the bowls in the sink, and turned on the TV.

The weather radar showed the storm was slowly

starting to move out of the area and the forecast was for the rain to slack off late tonight.

The clouds would hang around for another day or two with some wind and a few scattered showers. Temps would remain in the low sixties.

Anna approved. "Sounds like we'll be able to hit the beach tomorrow morning. As long as the road isn't flooded we can go out and do some detecting. Maybe we'll get lucky."

Remembering the coin the man had given me, I retrieved it from the cup holder and held it out for Anna to see.

35

"Is that the coin the old man gave you?"

"Yep."

"It's not a quarter."

"Nope."

"Do you know what it is?"

"Not sure. But I think it might be a coin from the treasure fleet."

Anna nodded, "Sure looks like it. But it might be a replica. They sell them in the museum over there."

I handed the coin to Anna. "Pick it up. Feel it. Look at it closely. Tell me if you think it is real or not."

Anna took the coin from my hand and examined it. "It sure feels real. And it looks hand-made, like the real ones do. And the color is right, too. Not shiny like a newer coin."

She continued, "The replicas they sell in the museum have the word 'copy' etched on the back. This one doesn't.

"So it could be real. But if it is real, it isn't a recent

find. It's been cleaned up a bit."

Anna held onto the coin, turning it over and over in her hand.

"So," I asked, "If it is real, what's it worth?"

She thought for a moment, then said, "Well it looks like it's silver, and it looks like an eight reale.

"I've seen eight reales from the Treasure Coast sell for about three hundred dollars. This one is in pretty good condition, so it might bring a bit more. Maybe even five hundred dollars."

I nodded. "So the guy gave us a pretty good reward for rescuing him."

"Yep," replied Anna. "But he gave it to you. Not me. It's yours Walker. Your lucky day."

I shook my head, "No, that's not the way it works. If it weren't for you, we wouldn't have been out there in the first place. So this coin is half yours."

Anna smiled, "That's pretty generous of you. You sure you want to do that?"

I nodded, "Yes, it's only fair. And anyway, when we go out to the beach tomorrow, I'm hoping we find a lot more like it."

Anna closed her hand around the coin, leaned forward and gave me a kiss on the cheek.

"What's that for?"

"Because you're a nice guy. Aren't many of them around these days."

36

Anna was still holding the coin when she asked, "When you found that guy on the beach, what was he doing?"

"It looked like," I replied, "he was trying to dig something up. He was scooping sand out of a hole, but the incoming waves kept filling the hole back in. When I grabbed him, he didn't want to leave. He said I had no idea what he'd found."

Anna nodded, "Maybe he discovered a treasure hoard. And maybe first thing tomorrow we should go and check that out.

"Think you can find that spot again?"

I nodded, "I'm pretty sure I can. It was right where the Indian River came up out of it's banks. And directly above where his car was parked.

"We should be able to locate it without much problem. But if the other guy is there in the morning, I don't want to bother him. It's his find, not ours."

Anna didn't reply. She just nodded thoughtfully.

37

It continued to rain hard all afternoon, so we spent the rest of the day inside, talking about treasure, looking at some of the maps I had found on the internet, and discussing our strategy for the next morning.

Anna suggested we put fresh batteries in our detectors and get everything ready for the hunt. Her plan was to get up at the break of dawn, grab a quick breakfast and head out to the beach.

Our first stop would be where we had seen the man and his dog. If we didn't find anything there, we'd go to the secret beach Anna had told me about earlier.

The rain finally stopped just after dark, and I suggested we go out on the beach and try some night detecting.

Anna said, "No. No detecting after dark. It's too dangerous after a storm like this one. The heavy rain and high tides can erode away a lot of sand, leaving cliffs instead of dunes.

"With those cliffs behind you, you may not be able

to get out of the way of big wave in the dark. You might end up being washed out to sea.

"It'll be better if we wait until the morning."

She had more experience doing this, so I didn't bother arguing.

After eating dinner, we watched TV for a few hours, and then prepared for bed.

As before, Anna slept on the couch, and I slept in the back bedroom.

Bob woke me about two hours after I hit the sack. He was out of food.

I filled his bowl and that seemed to settle him down. He ate a few bites, then went up front and snuggled in with Anna.

I guess he preferred sleeping with a woman.

I couldn't blame him. I preferred that as well.

I woke early the next morning. Well before sunrise. To me, it felt like Christmas morning with all the anticipation of what the day might bring.

As I lay there thinking about the treasures to be found, I heard Anna call out, "Walker, you awake?"

"Yep. Can't sleep."

"Well, get up then. You can cook me breakfast."

The power was still off and I didn't want to run the generator. This early in the morning it might disturb the few other people who had decided to ride out the storm in the campground

But since the the motorhome had a propane stove, I

was able to cook scrambled eggs and bacon without starting the generator.

Anna was impressed. A hot meal to start the day out right.

After breakfast, I checked Bob's food and water and made sure he was set for the day. He had decided to sleep in. Under the covers in my bed.

Up front, Anna was ready to go.

I made a final trip around the motorhome, making sure everything was locked up and that we had all the gear we needed.

The sun was just starting to peek over the clouds to the east when Anna and I loaded into the Land Cruiser and pulled out of the campsite.

When we reached A1A, we could see that most of the debris had been washed or blown off the road. It was easy going.

Anna drove south for about two miles, then slowed as we reached the general area where we had pulled the car out of the sand the day before.

The water from the Indian River had receded and things looked different today than they did yesterday.

She turned to me and said, "I'm not sure. Tell me when you think we're there."

Scanning the left shoulder of the road, I looked for the ruts in the sand that would have been left from yesterday's rescue.

Finally seeing them, I pointed and said, "Stop. This

is the spot."

Anna nodded, "Good eye. This is it."

Looking around, she said, "We don't want to park here. Other treasure hunters will see our car, and they may decide to join us.

"It'd be better if we park about a half mile down the road, behind the McLarty museum. It's got a paved lot, hidden from the main road. We can walk back up here from there."

I nodded, then said, "Maybe I should get out here, go on over the dune and wait for you. That way, we'll have the exact spot pin-pointed."

Anna agreed, "Good idea. You get out and go over the dune. I'll park, and walk back up to you.

"And Walker, don't find all the gold before I get there. Leave some for me."

I got out and grabbed my detector and scoop from the back. After I closed the door, Anna drove south toward the museum. Crossing the road, I followed the same trail up the dune I had followed the day before.

From the top of the dune I could see Anna had been right about the effect of the high tides on the beach.

Instead of the easy sloping sand dune that had been there the day before, the ocean side of the dune now dropped straight down about twelve feet to the beach.

The erosion had washed away much of the sand from the cliff face, exposing roots of trees long gone. These roots would be useful handholds as I worked my way down the sandy cliff face to the beach below.

With my detector and scoop slung over my shoulder, I climbed down the cliff face, marveling at how the storm had turned the soft dune into a sheer sandy cliff.

Upon reaching the beach, I could see that most of the soft white sand that had been there just two days before had been washed away. The beach surface now was a dark sandy field, strewn with rocks and bits of shells.

It was as if someone had used a road grader to scrape away the top layer of the beach. All the recent sand renourishment was for naught. The new sand, along with most of the old, was gone.

While waiting for Anna to make her way up the beach, I looked for any signs that would help me find the spot where the man had been digging the day before.

But I had no luck. The massive amount of erosion from the storm had removed too much sand. Any holes that he may have dug were long gone.

From behind I heard Anna say, "You didn't have to wait. You could have started detecting without me."

I shook my head. "No, you're the expert. Wanted to wait and hear your plan."

Anna pointed at the wall of sand that I had just climbed down, "Those roots and shells in the cliff are a good sign. It means the beach surface might be back to the level it was hundreds of years ago.

"There won't be bottle caps or pull tabs in this layer. Anything you find is going to be pretty old."

She looked up and down the beach, then said, "We should start at the base of the cliff and work parallel to the beach. We can do a hundred yard grid.

"You go north, I'll go south. After a hundred yards, move over six feet, turn around and come back here.

"We'll do that until we cover the whole beach.

"Before you start, turn off the iron discrimination on your detector. And dig every tone you get. No matter what you find, recover the target and put it in your pouch. And then refill the hole."

I nodded.

She smiled, "Good luck." Then she picked up her detector and scoop, turned and began her first hundred yard path to the south.

I turned north, and did the same.

Thirty yards in, I got my first hit.

38

I had been following the grid line Anna set out, swinging the detector slowly, trying to keep the coil an even distance from the surface.

Listening through the bulky headphones, I strained to hear the tell-tell tone that would indicate treasure.

For the first twenty yards, nothing. Not a single peep from the detector.

I was starting to think that either the detector wasn't working properly, or somehow I had fouled up the settings.

Just about the time I was going to go back to Anna and have her check the detector, the headphones chirped a loud tone. I had finally found something.

The readout on the detector's LCD display indicated an iron target about twelve inches below the surface.

I grabbed my scoop and removed six inches of sand above the spot indicated by the detector. Then I carefully sifted through the sand, looking for any signs of a metallic object.

Nothing.

I swung the detector back over the same spot, and got the tone again. The target was still buried under the surface.

I removed another six inches of sand. And this time, I could see a dark brown object at the bottom of the hole I'd dug.

Carefully positioning the scoop under the target, I was able to retrieve it in one piece.

Dumping the contents of the scoop onto the beach, I examined the item. It was about six inches long, heavily encrusted, looking like an iron railroad spike.

It wasn't gold or silver. But definitely was old, and perhaps even from the Spanish fleet.

My spirits buoyed by the discovery, I put the spike in my finds bag, filled the hole, and continued along the grid Anna had laid out for me.

Over the course of the next hour, I found several small objects, mostly iron flakes about the size of a potato chip. I also found a few heavily encrusted square headed nails.

As I reached the end of each hundred yard path, I'd turn around, move six feet closer to the waves, and head back in the direction I had just come.

This meant half of the time I could see Anna in the distance, and the other half I was facing away from her.

During the times I could see her, I watched as she swung her detector. Her motions were fluid, even graceful, much different than my own jerky, erratic swings.

Every few feet she would stop, swing the detector over a small area, then use her scoop to recover an item from the sand.

Based on the number of items she was retrieving, it looked like she was having a lot better luck than I was.

Other than the iron spike, I hadn't found anything of much interest. And my right elbow was starting to get sore from constantly swinging the detector.

At the end of one of my Anna facing grids, I turned back to the north and could see that the incoming tide was reducing the amount of remaining beach I needed to cover.

This made me happy. It meant we'd soon be taking a break as we repositioned for our next grid.

As I slowly detected up a grid line, I felt someone nudge me from behind. Thinking it was Anna, I turned with a smile, hoping she was announcing we were going to take a break.

But it wasn't Anna. It was something else. Something totally unexpected.

39

Anna was still far in the distance, walking a grid line away from me.

And in front of me sat a dog.

A big black Labrador Retriever.

He had come up and nudged me from behind, then he stood still, wagging his tail, waiting for me to pet him.

The strangest part was I had seen the dog before.

It was Jake. The black lab from the car we had rescued during the storm.

And if Jake was here, his owner should be close by.

I scanned up and down the beach, but the only other person I could see was Anna. She was about a hundred yards south, detecting a grid line away from me.

I turned back to Jake, rubbed his head, and said, "You lost?"

He backed up a few feet, then dipped down on his front legs and barked at me. Like he wanted to play.

That was fine with me since I needed a break from swinging the detector.

I found a piece of driftwood and tossed it over his head. As it sailed over, he sat motionless, staring at me.

Apparently he didn't want to play stick. He wanted to play something else.

Jake got down on his front legs with his rear end up in the air, his tail wagging wildly. He barked at me, then jumped up and ran twenty feet down the beach and sat.

I said, "Sorry, Jake. I don't know that game." I picked up my detector, and started back on my grid line.

Jake didn't like this. He got up and ran back to me and barked. He wanted my attention.

"What is Jake? Has Timmy fallen in the well?"

Jake looked at me, cocking his head to the side, as if he were trying to figure out what I had said.

Then he barked, turned and ran to the same spot he had before. But this time, instead of sitting, he used his front paws to dig a small hole.

He barked at me again, and I swear he nodded at the hole.

"Okay, I get it. You want me to dig in the hole."

I walked to the spot where Jake was sitting, and ran my detector across the hole he had dug. Nothing. Not even a peep.

"Sorry, Jake. There's nothing there, buddy."

Turning around, I headed back to my grid line.

But Jake wasn't going to let me off that easy. He jumped up and barked at me again.

I turned and could see he was digging furiously in the hole. Then he stopped and sat. Waiting for my return.

"Okay, Jake. I'll give it another shot."

I walked back and swung the detector coil over the deeper hole that Jake had dug. And this time, I got a beep.

There was something metal in the hole.

I scooped out the first six inches of sand, and swung the detector over the hole again. A louder beep this time.

Definitely something down there.

Using the scoop, I dug down another twelve inches. Then swung the detector over the hole, and it beeped louder.

The readout on the detector's LCD display showed the target had the potential of being silver, and was at least twelve inches below the detector coil.

The hole was now twenty inches deep, and the wet sand on the sides was starting to cave in. To get to the buried item, I'd have to widen the hole, then dig deeper.

I unhooked my detector and laid it on the sand. Using my sand scoop like a shovel, I started enlarging the hole. I continued until the pit was about three feet across and two feet deep.

I picked up the detector and swung it in the bottom of the pit. This time it beeped much louder.

Jake barked again. I was getting closer.

40

"Well Jake, I don't know how you did it, but it looks like you may have found treasure."

Jake looked up at me and started wagging his tail. I stepped over and patted him on the head.

"You're a good dog, Jake."

He leaned into my hand and had what looked like a smile on his face. If you've had a dog, you've probably seen that look.

"Jake, where's your owner? He's probably looking for you."

Once again, Jake cocked his head as if he were trying to understand what I was saying.

Then Jake's ears came to attention, like he was hearing something in the distance. He swiveled his head and apparently seeing the source of the sound, he took off like a shot, kicking up sand as he ran north.

Watching Jake, I could see he was heading toward someone up the beach. About two hundred yards away, a man with a metal detector had stepped out of the dunes.

I couldn't be sure, but from this distance the man looked like he might have been the same one we had rescued the day before.

When Jake reached the man, he stopped and sat. The man gave Jake a pat on the head, then looked at me, waved, and gave me a thumbs-up signal.

He and Jake then turned and walked north. Away from me.

I figured that by giving me the thumbs up, Jake's owner was saying it was okay to detect this part of the beach.

After they walked out of sight, I returned my attention to the pit I'd dug with Jake's guidance.

Using my scoop, I carefully removed six inches of sand from the bottom of what was now a three foot deep pit. Then I swung the detector coil inside the pit.

The detector responded with multiple tones. It's LCD display showed several target items below.

Fearing that using the metal scoop might damage the targets, I stepped down into the pit and started removing sand with my hands.

After digging for about a minute, I felt something solid. Perhaps the treasure I'd been looking for.

Using my fingers, I drew an outline around the edges of the object buried below. This would be my guide to how much sand I needed to remove before I could retrieve it.

The outline showed that the object was larger than I expected. About the size of a softball.

I continued to brush away the sand until I got a better look at what I was dealing with.

At first glance it looked like a bone, but after removing more sand, I could see the telltale outline and ridges of a large clam shell.

Finding shells on the beach is not unusual. In fact it is to be expected. But finding shells that cause a metal detector to sound a tone? That's different.

I removed more sand, and saw that instead of finding a single shell, I'd found a circle of large clam shells, all face down.

The way the shells were arranged seemed to suggest they they had been put this way on purpose.

Maybe there was something under the shells.

I sure hoped so.

Using my hands to dig a small groove around the largest shell, I reached under and carefully nudged it out of its resting place. To my surprise, rather than being just the top of a clam shell, it was the top and bottom. Creating a protective cover around whatever was inside.

Opening the shell, I found a clump of dime sized coins that had corroded together.

I shook my head in disbelief.

I had found Spanish treasure.

And judging by the number of shells in the pit, there was more.

I carefully put the clump of coins into my finds

bag, and returned my attention to the other shells in the pit.

Removing the top of the second shell, I found another clump of silver coins. Almost the same size of the first clump.

I carefully put these in my finds bag with the first clump.

Back down in the pit, I removed another large shell. This one held three gold coins, each about the size of a quarter. They looked newly minted. No signs of wear or corrosion.

If these were truly gold, they would worth quite a bit.

I wrapped each of these coins with tissues from the packet of Kleenex I carried in my belly pack, then put them in my top right shirt pocket.

Back in the pit, I removed the final shell, and inside it I found a large gold ring with a bright green stone in the center.

The ring appeared to be hand hammered, with carved initials on one side, and a family crest on the other.

As with the gold coins, I carefully wrapped the ring in tissues, then put it in my other shirt pocket, making sure the pocket was securely buttoned.

From what I could see, it appeared that someone had dug a deep pit on the beach, placed a layer of large clam shells in the bottom of the pit, and then placed something of value in each of the shells.

They then covered each shell with a matching top, either to hide the treasures from prying eyes, or to protect them from the elements.

Whatever the reason, the two layers of shells had worked surprisingly well to keep the treasure in good condition for however long it had been buried here.

Looking into the pit, I wondered if there could be another layer of shells in the sand below the first.

To find out, I grabbed my detector and swung it into the pit. The detector responded with multiple tones. That meant there were still metal objects buried below.

As I turned to put my detector back on the sand, I saw that Anna was coming my way. She had her head down watching the sand in front of her feet as she followed her grid line.

I picked up my sand scoop and began swinging it wildly over my head. Hoping to get her attention.

41

At first, Anna didn't see me.

I was standing above my treasure pit, trying to get her attention and hoping I didn't attract the attention of others on the beach. I didn't need strangers knowing I had found a pit filled with lost treasure.

Finally, she looked up and saw me. She smiled and waved. Then realizing that I was trying to get her attention, she cocked her head to the side, as if questioning what I was trying to say.

Using my right hand, I motioned for her to come join me. She understood immediately. Taking her headphones off, she walked quickly toward me.

As she got close enough for me to hear her, she asked, "You find something?"

I grinned and said, "You're not going to believe this."

I reached into my bag and retrieved the small clump of silver coins.

She stepped closer and said, "Wow! That's pretty good."

Still grinning like a fool, I said, "There's more."

I retrieved the second stack of coins and held them out for her to see.

Her eyes widened. "You found these, too? Where?"

I pointed to the pit behind me. "Down there. But that's not all I found."

Reaching into my shirt pocket I retrieved one of the gold coins.

"You found gold? Gold?"

I nodded. "Yes, and not just the one coin. I found three."

I put the gold coin back into my pocket, and retrieved the ring I'd found and held it out for Anna to see.

"And I found this."

Anna leaned over to get a closer look at the ring. "Can I hold it?"

I nodded yes.

She picked it up, felt it's weight, and then turned the ring so that the green stone caught the light of the sun.

Looking at me she whispered, "Do you know what this is? It's an emerald."

Handing the ring back she said, "Walker, you did really, really good. Where did you find all this?"

I pointed to the pit behind me, "Right there. Thanks to Jake."

42

"Jake? Who's Jake?" asked Anna.

I smiled. "You remember the car we pulled out of the sand yesterday during the storm?"

"Yes . . ."

"Well, Jake was the big black dog that was in the car."

Anna looked confused, "So what does the dog have to do with this treasure?"

I told her the story.

"Jake showed up earlier, and herded me over to this spot. He made me dig here."

"He made you dig? How'd he do that?"

"I was detecting my grid line, and Jake came and sat in front of me. And when I tried to get him to move, he wouldn't. Then he barked kind of like he was saying 'follow me'. "

Anna nodded.

"Then he came over to this spot and dug a small hole. He seemed to be telling me to dig here. So I dug.

And I found the treasure."

Anna rubbed her head, "So you're saying that the dog led you to treasure?"

"That's exactly what I'm saying. And more importantly, now that you're here you can take your turn digging in this pit."

"What do you mean?"

"I mean, I dug the first layer and retrieved all this. But according to my detector, there's more down there.

"I've found my treasure. Now it's your turn."

Anna smiled, then looked at the ocean. "The tide's coming in pretty fast. This pit will be under water in less than an hour. We've got to hurry."

She swung her detector in the pit and smiled when the resulting tone indicated gold below.

But instead of climbing down into the pit, she paused and said, "I don't feel right about this. You found this treasure, so you should be digging it, not me. It's rightfully yours."

I shook my head, "That's not the way I see it. Jake found this. And since we were both involved in Jake's rescue, you deserve whatever you find down there.

"And you better hurry, the tide's coming in fast."

Anna nodded, "Okay, as long as you're sure."

I pointed to the ocean, and then pointed to the pit. "Dig!"

Anna climbed down into the pit and started removing the layer of shells below the ones I'd already dug out.

Sifting her hands through the softly packed wet sand, I could see that she'd found something. Gently she retrieved the object, brushed off the sand, and held it up for me to see.

It appeared to be half dollar sized coin. The sea water had tarnished it to almost solid black in color, but it was clearly silver. A Spanish silver coin.

Anna kept digging, and over the next thirty minutes, she found seven more silver coins, a badly bent silver fork, and a heavily encrusted silver cross.

The incoming tide was bringing the waves closer and closer and seawater was starting to spill over into the pit.

"Anna, we don't have much longer before the waves reach us. You need to get out of there soon."

"Not yet. Hand me my detector. I want to be sure we've gotten everything."

I handed her the detector and she swung it in the pit. It beeped.

"It's showing there's still gold down here. I'm going to find it."

Anna handed me the detector, then she crouched down in the pit, digging with both hands. As she dug, small streams of water from the incoming tide began filling the bottom of the pit.

Ignoring the water, Anna kept digging. But she wouldn't be able to dig much longer. The tide was coming in fast, and waves were starting to circle the pit.

As the sand around the top of the pit became soaked, it began to crumble and slide down around Anna's feet.

"Anna, you need to get out of there. The tide is coming in pretty fast."

"Two more minutes! That's all I need."

A large wave crashed over the pit, splashing a slurry of wet sand down onto Anna. She ignored it and kept digging.

Grabbing our detectors, I carried them up the beach away from incoming tide. Then I came back to haul Anna out of the pit, whether she wanted to come out or not.

As I reached the edge of the pit, Anna stood up, triumphantly holding gold coins in her clenched fist.

"Got them! Now help me out."

I reached for her and we locked arms, wrist over wrist.

The walls of the pit were saturated and the wet sand under Anna's feet collapsed with each step as she tried to climb her way out.

The harder she scrambled, the faster the sand filled in the hole. It quickly covered her feet, then her ankles. The heavy, slushy mix inched up toward her knees with each fresh wave.

If wet sand filled to her waist, the suction would make it impossible to get her out of the pit. In minutes, her head would be underwater.

We both knew this. I planted my feet and leaned back, struggling to pull her out.

I realized that each time a wave washed over us, there was a moment when the water would soften the sand enough to pull Anna a few more inches further out of the pit.

Timing our efforts with these waves, me pulling with both arms and her pushing with both feet, I finally dragged her over the edge and onto the beach.

Almost immediately, the pit collapsed and filled in with wet sand. Just a few feet away, Anna lay sprawled on the beach, her breath ragged.

She looked up at me and smiled. Then she opened her tightly closed fist revealing three gold coins and said, "We found treasure!"

I helped Anna stand, and we gathered up our detecting gear. Based on the speed of the incoming tide, Anna reckoned we had less than thirty minutes before the entire beach would be under water.

We were both soaking wet, covered with sand, and weighed down with detecting gear and treasure. We knew the walk back to the Cruiser would be slow and difficult.

But our spirits were lifted by the treasure we had found, and we quickly made our way down the beach. After twenty minutes, Anna pointed at something high up on the dune ahead.

The wooden skeleton of a Spanish Galleon.

43

I stared in disbelief. There was no way a Spanish Galleon should be here on the beach. The wood would have rotted away long ago.

Anna shook her head, "It's not what you think. It's a replica. Put there by the people who run the McLarty treasure museum.

"That ship tells us we've reached the walkover to the museum. And that's where I parked the Cruiser."

I was too tired to reply. And happy that we were leaving the incoming tide and beach behind.

When we reached Anna's Land Cruiser, we unloaded our gear into the back, wiped the sand off our clothes and got in.

Anna spoke first, "Where to?"

"How about this," I replied. "Let's go back to the campground and clean up. And then we can get something to eat."

Anna smiled, "Sounds good to me."

Back at the park entrance, we were greeted by a ranger who advised us that the park power was back on and that we could move back to our riverfront site whenever we wanted.

I was happy to hear this. Even though our new campsite by the restrooms offered protection from the wind during the storm, it also had distinct outhouse odor.

When we got back to the motorhome, Bob greeted us at the door with a very loud "Meoooow." He was either happy to see us, or wanted food.

I went back and checked his bowls. They were both nearly full. I guess he was just happy to see us.

Back up front, Anna had spread a layer of paper towels on the dining table. On top of the towels she was arranging her finds for the day.

Three gold coins, eight silver coins, the broken silver fork, and a small silver cross.

I nodded, "Pretty impressive."

She smiled, "We did good today. We found gold and silver coins. And Spanish artifacts. All from that one honey hole. Pretty amazing!"

I smiled. "Yeah, thanks to Jake."

Anna looked at me and said, "Do you really think Jake knew there was treasure there? Or was it just a lucky coincidence?"

I shook my head, "I don't know. He was pretty insistent I dig in that one spot. He acted like he knew there was something there.

"So I guess it's possible. Dogs have been trained to

find lots of things. Maybe Jake has a nose for gold and silver."

Anna smiled, "If he does, I'd sure like to follow him around."

"Yeah," I said. "Me too!"

Anna sorted her treasure and carefully wrapped each item in a paper towel, then put them in her overnight bag.

When she was done, I put out fresh paper towels and laid my treasures on top.

I'd found three gold coins, two stacks of Spanish silver coins, and the big gold ring with the green stone.

Not bad for a morning on the beach.

Anna looked over my finds and said, "That ring is unbelievable. No telling what it's worth."

Then she asked, "You ready for lunch?"

I was. As I wrapped up my treasures, Anna rummaged through the fridge and came out with everything she needed to make us turkey sandwiches.

After eating I asked, "So, what about the rest of the day? We going back out on the beach?"

Shaking her head, she said, "According to the tide charts, high tide won't be for another three hours.

"That means the beach will be pretty much under water until around seven this evening. So, unless you want to go back out after dark, detecting is over for the day."

I nodded. "That's okay with me. I'm a little tired.

Not sure if I want to go out again.

"And since the ranger said we can move back to our original campsite, maybe we ought to do that. Then if you want, we can go into town and get some more supplies."

Smiling, Anna said, "Sounds like a good plan to me."

Then she asked, "How long you plan on staying here in the campground?"

I thought a moment, then replied, "My original plan was to stay through Saturday. Today is Tuesday, which means at least four more days. How about you? How long are you staying?"

She smiled, "It depends. How much longer are you going to let me sleep on your couch?"

44

After lunch, I cleaned up and took the trash bag outside to the nearest container. While outside, I checked the campground showers and was happy to see that the water had been turned back on.

Back inside, I announced my findings and told Anna I was going to take a hot shower in the campground bathroom, then move the motorhome back to the original campsite.

Anna said she too would be taking a shower, and suggested I lock the motorhome while we were out, since we both had treasures worth stealing.

I agreed, and before heading to the showers, I put my treasure finds in the small safe I kept under the bed in the back. The same place I kept my gun.

With our treasures secure, I locked the motorhome and we headed toward the showers, agreeing to meet back at the campsite in twenty minutes.

The men's side of the campground bathroom had two shower stalls with locking doors. Both were empty, so I took the far stall and locked the door behind me.

Stripping down, I turned on the water and stepped into the shower. At first, the water was cold, but soon warmed up and turned hot.

It felt great, relieving some of the aches in my elbow and shoulders I'd gotten from swinging the detector all morning.

I took my time in the shower, letting the steaming water rinse away the dirt and sand I'd accumulated during our morning adventure.

After about ten minutes, I turned off the water and grabbed a towel. As I was drying off, Anna called from the bathroom door, "Walker, you still in there?"

"Yep, be out in a minute."

She shouted back, "If you like, I could come and join you."

I hesitated, then said, "Sure, come on it. I don't know how the other guys in here would feel, but it's fine with me."

I was bluffing. While taking a shower with Anna sounded like fun, I wasn't sure it'd be the right thing to do. Not until I knew where I stood with Sarah.

Instead of waiting for her, I quickly dressed and headed out the door.

She was standing outside, drying her hair with a towel.

I smiled and asked, "How was your shower?"

"Lonely. How was yours?"

"Mine was great. The water was hot and it felt good

to finally wash off all that sand."

I turned toward the motorhome, "You ready?"

"You bet!" she replied.

After unlocking the door, Anna followed me into the motorhome and we hung our wet clothes on the shower rod in the bathroom.

Back up front, I asked, "You ready to move back to our original campsite?"

"Sure, if you are."

"I'm ready. But I need to bring the slide in. Think you can hold Bob for a few minutes?"

Bob was already at Anna's feet, rubbing against her ankles. She bent over and picked him up.

Once the slide was safely in, I did a quick check to make sure everything inside was secure. I didn't want anything crashing to the floor once I got the motorhome moving.

While I made these preparations, Anna sat at the dinette table, petting Bob and watching me.

When I was finished, she asked, "Are you mad at me?"

"No, not at all. Why do you ask?"

"Well, since our shower, you haven't said much. I hope I didn't embarrass you."

"Anna, it's nothing like that. I'm just tired from swinging the detector all morning. But I'm looking forward to our trip into town, assuming you still want to go."

Anna smiled, "Yes, I still want to go. I need to get some food. And a new tent. Mine blew away in the storm."

I shook my head, "Anna, you don't need a tent. You can stay here as long as you want."

"I know, but it's better if I have my own place. You might be getting tired of me."

"Not a chance. I like having you around. And so does Bob."

She smiled, "That's nice to know. But I still need to replace my tent and sleeping bag. I'll need them after you leave."

I nodded, "I guess you're right. But you're welcome to stay here, even if you get a new tent."

She walked over and gave me a hug, then headed for the door. "I need to move the Land Cruiser before you can move the motorhome. I'll meet you at the old campsite."

She walked out the door, leaving me and Bob behind. He looked up a me, blinked his eyes and said, "Murrph."

Apparently Bob didn't like seeing Anna leave. He liked having her around. I guess I did too.

I said to him, "Bob, we're going to be moving in a minute. You might want to get somewhere safe."

Seeing me sit down in the driver's seat, Bob ran to the back. I started the motorhome and drove down to our original campsite, then carefully backed onto the parking pad.

Going outside, I connected the power and water hookups, and made sure there was plenty of room for the slide-out.

Back inside, I grabbed Bob, and while holding him, I ran the slide-room out. Bob was always fascinated when the slide went out, especially if it meant the windows above the couch gave him a perch where he could watch birds and squirrels.

Today was his lucky day. Birds fluttered in the small oaks that lined the side of our campsite. Bob was soon on the top of the couch, watching them.

His little bump of a tail would flick when a bird came tantalizingly close. Even though Bob was an inside cat, his instincts were still from the jungle.

As I was admiring Bob, Anna knocked on the door.

"Come on in."

I pointed to the dinette and said, "Sit."

She sat.

"Anna, let's clear the air. I don't want there to be any bad feelings between us. Especially on the day we both found amazing treasures on the beach."

She smiled uncertainly.

"So here's the deal. I may have a girlfriend back in Englewood. I may not. I guess I won't be sure until I get back."

"Until then, I'm not going to fool around and risk losing her. I hope you understand."

Anna nodded, then said, "What makes you think

I'm interested in fooling around with you?

"If it's because of that comment back at the showers, you can just forget it. Because that was a joke.

"And anyway, I'm not the kind of girl that fools around with someone I just met."

I nodded. Then smiled big.

"Okay then. It's settled. No fooling around."

Then I said, "We found treasure today. Let's go into town, get some food, maybe something to drink, and come back here and celebrate."

She grinned, "I can't believe how lucky you are. You get rescued by a beautiful woman. Then a stranger gives you a valuable silver coin. Then a dog leads you to a horde of gold and silver treasure.

"You've got be the luckiest guy on the planet."

I nodded, "Yeah, I've heard that before."

She smiled, "Okay, Mr Lucky. Let's go to town, get some supplies, then come back here and celebrate."

And that's what we did.

45

Before we left for town, Anna retrieved her gym bag and took it out to the Land Cruiser. Still inside, I checked on Bob, then locked up the motorhome. Didn't want anyone breaking in to steal my Spanish treasures, or bothering Bob.

Out in the Land Cruiser, Anna was ready to go. I jumped in, and we headed out.

We were both pretty happy. We'd found treasure. Gold and silver. And the day had gone well.

Anna drove the eighteen miles down A1A toward Vero beach, then turned right toward the highway 60 bridge that crossed the intracoastal waterway and the Indian River.

We caught the red light, and while stopped, Anna said, "Looks like the bridge is open. That's good."

I nodded.

When the light turned green, Anna headed over the bridge. From my side, I could look down over the bridge railing and see several boats that had broken their moorings and ended up beached on the sandbars below.

I was happy not to have been in a boat during the storm. It wouldn't have been pleasant.

At the bottom of the bridge, Anna turned left, then followed highway 60 through the city of Vero.

As she slowed for another stop light she said, "There's three places I want to go.

"WalMart to get a tent and sleeping bag. Publix to get food. And right up here, Ken's Coins."

Anna pulled into a small strip mall and parked in front of a store with black metal security grates on the windows and doors.

A small overhead sign read, "Ken's Coins. We buy gold and silver."

Anna grabbed her gym bag and got out of the Cruiser. Turning back to me she said, "Come on in. You'll find this interesting."

I got out and followed her to the store's front door. A sign on the door read, 'ring buzzer for service.'

Above the door, a small security camera was mounted so that it would capture the image of anyone pressing the buzzer.

Anna buzzed and a few moments later a man's voice came from the speaker above the door.

"What can I help you with?"

Anna looked up toward the camera and said, "Ken, it's me, Anna. I've got a coin I want to show you."

There was no response from the speaker, but the

door buzzed and we heard the bolt unlock.

Anna opened the door and we went in. The door closed behind us, and the deadbolt locked electronically.

Inside, the store was narrow, probably no more than fifteen feet wide. A glass display case at the back, separated the public area from the employees. Behind it, a wall of mirrors, with a doorway leading into a small office.

While we waiting for the proprietor to join us, I examined the items in the glass display case.

It held a selection of gold and silver coins, with dates ranging from the current year to as far back as the 1600's.

In addition to the coins, the case contained rings, necklaces, gold chains, and several iron artifacts.

I looked up as a short, slightly overweight man with a stubby cigar in his mouth walked out of the back room.

His white shirt barely contained his belly, and his suspenders were working hard to keep his pants up off the ground.

Over his shoulder, a black leather holster held a shiny pistol that looked to be a Smith & Wesson 357 revolver.

The gun was likely a must-have for one who made his living buying and selling rare gold and silver coins these days.

When the man saw Anna, he smiled. "Anna, long

time no see. You doing all right?"

"Doing fine. How about you? I see you're still smoking those cigars."

"Naw, the wife won't let me smoke them any more. But I can still chew on the unlit ones."

Ken removed the unlit but soggy cigar from his mouth and placed it in a clean ashtray on his side of the counter.

"So, who's this guy?" Ken said, pointing to me.

Anna smiled, "This is Walker. I'm taking care of him for a few days."

Ken looked at me, then back at Anna, "This one looks better than the last one. Hope you don't have to shoot him, too."

Anna smiled, "Walker doesn't know about that. Let's keep it that way."

Then she said, "Ken, I've got a coin I want to show you."

She reached into her gym bag and pulled out one of the gold coins she had found on the beach. She placed the coin on the rubber mat that sat in the center of the glass counter, directly in front of Ken.

Sitting down on a swivel stool on his side of the counter, Ken looked up at Anna and said, "May I?"

She nodded.

He picked up the coin, and using a jeweler's loupe, inspected it closely. After a few moments, he turned the coin over and examined the back.

Then he placed the coin back down on the rubber mat, and reached behind him to retrieve a large reference book.

Flipping through the book, he found the page he was looking for.

"This is a nice coin. Looks like an eight escudos from the 1715 fleet. Dated 1712 from the Lima mint. The condition is almost fine, very little wear.

"According to the book, this coin has a retail value of around twelve thousand dollars."

Anna smiled.

Ken continued, "The book was printed last year, so these values are out of date. Could be worth more. Or could be worth less. Let's check the internet to see what they've recently sold for."

He rolled his stool down to a computer screen and tapped a few keys. Then waited.

"Okay, here it is. An eight escudo, dated 1712 from the Lima mint in good condition, recently sold at auction for thirteen five.

"So retail is probably twelve thousand. If you want to sell it today, I can give you sixty five hundred for it. Cash."

Anna shook her head. "Ken, I know you've got to make a profit, but you can do better than that. Maybe nine thousand?"

Shaking his head, he said, "No way. But I'll do seven thousand. And that's it. No more."

Anna didn't say anything. Instead, she reached into her gym bag and pulled out the second gold coin, and put it next to the one already on the counter.

Ken looked at Anna, "So, there's two of them?"

He picked up the second coin and examined it. "This one is as good as the first. Same date and mint."

Then he said, "I'll give you fourteen thousand for both."

Anna looked over at me. I raised my eyebrows in reply.

Ken could see that Anna was hesitating. "Okay Anna, what else do you have in the bag? Maybe we can add it to your collection here."

Anna reached back into her bag and brought out the third gold coin. Then reaching back in, she brought out the rest. Seven silver coins, the broken silver fork, and the small silver cross.

Ken whistled and said, "Wow. Looks like you had a good day."

He picked up the silver cross first. "This I want. I'll give you twelve hundred for it."

Then he looked at the other items. "Four hundred for the fork. Three fifty each for the silver coins. And the same as before for the gold coin."

He got out his calculator and totaled it up.

"Twenty five thousand for everything. Cash."

46

Anna nodded. "You've got a deal."

Ken smiled, "Wait right here. I'll write this up and bring you your money." He stood and stepped through the door to his office, leaving Anna and me alone in the front of the store.

She turned to me and whispered, "Can you believe that? Twenty five thousand dollars!"

Then she leaned in and gave me a hug. I hugged her back.

Ken walked in while we were still embraced. He smiled and said, "None of that in here. Get a room."

He had a pen in his right hand, a single sheet of paper in his left, and in his front pants pocket, a red bank bag.

He placed the sheet of paper on the glass counter in front of Anna and handed her a pen, "Sign this, stating you didn't steal those coins, then we can settle up."

Anna picked up the document, read it, and then signed.

Ken took the document and handed Anna the

money bag.

She unzipped it, to reveal five banded stacks of one hundred dollar bills. Each band was marked 'five thousand'.

Ken pointed at the money, "Each stack contains fifty bills. Count them before you leave."

Anna quickly counted the bills in each stack. Then said, "Twenty five thousand dollars. It's all there."

She put the stacks of bills back into the bank bag, zipped it up, and dropped the bank bag into her gym bag.

Turning to me, Ken asked, "What about you, Walker? Anything you want to show me?"

I shook my head, "Not today. Maybe later."

"Well, when you get ready to sell, come see me. I'll treat you right.

"And Anna, be careful carrying that much money. People do bad things for a whole lot less."

Anna nodded, "Don't worry about me Ken. You know what happened to the last guy who tried something."

We walked toward the door and Ken buzzed us out. Anna looked around to make sure the coast was clear, then she quickly walked to the Land Cruiser.

I followed.

As we pulled out of the parking lot, I asked, "What'd Ken mean about not shooting me. Is there something I should know?"

Anna kept her eyes on the road and said, "It's nothing. Just an inside joke."

47

After leaving Ken's, Anna drove to the nearest Walmart where she bought a tent and sleeping bag to replace the ones that had blown away during the storm.

After Walmart, we went to the big Publix grocery store, where Anna picked out our celebratory dinner. Steaks, salad, and two bottles of red wine.

From Publix we headed back to Hutchinson Island and our campsite at Sebastian Inlet State Park.

On the way, Anna pointed to the cars parked on the side of the road, "Probably treasure hunters. Now that the bridge is open, we'll see a lot more of them.

"And there will probably be a lot more people in the campground too. That means we'll have to be careful and not let anyone know what we found. People do crazy things when they think you have gold and cash."

I nodded, "You're right. We'll keep this just between you and me."

When we reached the park gate, the ranger waved us through. After being in the park for almost a week, he recognized Anna's Land Cruiser.

Back at the campsite, Anna picked up her gym bag and said, "If you don't mind, I'm going to keep this in the motorhome until I find a safer place. I don't want to risk leaving it here in the Cruiser or the tent."

Inside the motorhome, Bob came trotting from the back and then stopped to stretch. He was happy to see us, but didn't want us to know. Cats are funny that way.

He sat and said, "Murrrph."

Anna reached down and rubbed his ear. "Bob, you sure are a handsome cat. I'm trusting you to keep this bag safe. Can you do that?"

Bob butted Anna's leg with his head and said, "Murrrph."

Which meant yes, he'd keep the bag safe. As long as Anna continued to rub his ears at least once a day.

I brought the food in from the Cruiser and put it on the counter. Then asked, "So, when do you want to eat?"

Anna looked up, "A bit later. I want to put my tent up first, make sure I've got a place to sleep tonight."

I said, "Anna, stay here tonight. There's plenty of room."

She nodded, "Yeah, I know. And I appreciate the offer. I might take you up on it. But, I'll feel better if I have the option to stay in my own place."

She gave Bob one last rub, stood up and walked to the door. She turned to me and said, "Leave the steaks out. Make sure Bob doesn't get them."

She opened the door and stepped out.

I looked at Bob and said, "If you can figure them out, you're doing better than me."

Now that I was back in the motorhome alone, I decided to check my phone to see if I had missed any calls.

It'd been four days since I last spoken with Sarah. Maybe she'd called.

I checked and there were no messages, no missed calls. She hadn't called. So I decided to call her.

I punched in her number, and after five rings, a man answered.

"Hello?"

"Yes, may I speak to Sarah?"

"Sorry, she's not available."

"Uh, you have her phone? Is she with you?"

"Look, she's not available. You want to leave a message?"

"Not really. I'm just checking in on her. Making sure she's okay."

"Oh, she's doing great. If you want to leave a message, I can tell her you called."

"No, never mind. I'll call back later." I hung up.

What was that all about? Why wasn't Sarah answering her phone? And who was the guy on the other end?

Maybe I really didn't want to know.

48

After the call, I went back to the bedroom and checked to make sure my treasure finds were still there.

They were.

Then I started thinking about the reasons Sarah wouldn't be answering her phone. And why her phone would be answered by a man.

The only reason I could think of was she had a guest and she was out of the room when the phone rang. And he was comfortable enough with her to answer her phone.

Maybe a relative? I could call Sarah's sister Molly, and she might know.

But did I really want to do that? Maybe I'd be better off not knowing.

While I was pondering this, Anna knocked on the door, "Walker, it's time to celebrate!"

I met her at the door, and she gave me another big hug.

"What's with the hugging?" I asked.

She smiled, "I feel good. We found treasure today. And that money is really going to make things easier for me.

"It means I don't have to worry about finding a job right away. It's like a big weight has been lifted. So I'm happy. And I'm going to celebrate. I'll probably hug you three or four more times before the evening's over."

She smiled and walked to the kitchen counter.

Pointing at the steaks, she said, "I was thinking we could cook these outside on the grill. Drink a little wine, and watch the sun go down over the river."

I nodded. "Sounds good to me. What do you want me to do?"

She pointed to the wine, "I'll do the cooking. You open the wine."

Grabbing the bag of charcoal we'd purchased earlier, Anna headed outside to the grill. I was pretty sure she was humming a happy tune.

Opening the bottle of wine, I poured us both a glass, and followed her outside.

I watched as she built a small pyramid of charcoal in the campground grill. She stuffed a crumbled up paper towel at the bottom as kindling for her fire.

Lighting a match to the paper, she soon had flames under the charcoal.

Anna nursed the fire for a few minutes, blowing on the flames trying to get the charcoal briquettes to light up. It took only a few minutes before the charcoal was glowing.

After she was satisfied with her fire, she turned to me and said, "Okay. It looks like we'll be grilling in about twenty minutes. In the meantime, we can drink a little wine, and you can tell me more about why you're living in a motorhome."

We sipped our wine as I told my story.

I had been the head of computer operations for a large manufacturing plant. The company that owned the plant decided to move it to Mexico. They announced they were closing the plant, laying off all the people who worked there, including me.

The day they announced the plant closing, my wife unexpectedly filed for divorce.

It was a friendly divorce. We split everything we owned right down the middle. It wasn't a lot, but we both ended up with a little money in the bank. I also got to keep my last paycheck and severance pay.

Using that little bit of money, I traded my pickup truck for the motorhome and had been living in it ever since.

Anna smiled, "Quite a story. So what's it like living in a motorhome? And where do you stay when you're not in a campground like this one."

I laughed. "Before I got the motorhome, I lived in a tent for two weeks. Compared to that, the motorhome is a palace. It's got everything I need, and I can take it anywhere."

"Until recently I've been parking in the backyard of the girl I mentioned before. She hasn't been charging me rent. So other than buying food, it hasn't cost me much."

Anna took a sip of her wine. "What if the girl decides you need to move? What will you do then?"

Until just a few days ago, I hadn't even thought about this possibility. Would Sarah soon ask me to park my motorhome somewhere else?

My gut was saying 'yes'. Eventually, maybe soon, she'd want me to find some other place to live.

I sighed, "When that happens, I guess I'll have to find another friend to stay with. Or maybe buy a vacant lot where I can park the motorhome."

Anna nodded, then said, "Maybe you could buy a RV park. That way, you'd always have a place to stay, and you could invite your friends who have motorhomes and trailers to stay at your park.

"If you did that, I could come visit you."

I smiled. She was right, owning a small RV park might be fun.

Anna got up and tended to her fire, then went inside the motorhome to get the steaks.

Back outside she put the steaks on the grill, then said, "I'm going back in to make a salad. You stay out here and make sure the fire doesn't flare up."

She placed a large steak fork on the table in front of me, and went back inside the motorhome.

A few minutes later she came back out with a large bowl of salad, two plates, and eating utensils.

She checked the steaks, and being satisfied with their progress, sat at the table facing me. "You're not smiling. We're supposed to be celebrating. Something wrong?"

49

Yes, there was something wrong. I'd called Sarah and a man answered.

Instead of sharing this bit of information with Anna, I said, "Just thinking about my living arrangements back in Englewood. And how I might need to find another place."

Anna reached out and touched my hand, "You can worry about that some other time. Right now we're going to eat and start our celebration. So pour some more wine and let's celebrate today's good fortune."

I poured and we drank and ate and drank some more. The meal was excellent, and the steak was just what we needed after eating microwave meals for so many days in a row.

After we'd finished, I cleaned away the plates and asked, "How about we take a walk?"

Anna said, "Sure. A walk sounds good."

I locked the motorhome and we headed out. Anna's campsite was right next to mine, and as we passed it, she pointed at her tent and said, "That's where I'm sleeping tonight."

"What about our celebration?" I asked. "You should sleep in the motorhome tonight. You know the couch will be more comfortable than sleeping on the ground in your tent."

Anna smiled, "We'll see."

We continued our walk through the park, and eventually made it to the fishing pier that stretched out over the Atlantic ocean.

The conditions were far different than when I had first walked on the pier. The weather was calm, the decking was dry. It no longer felt dangerous.

Hard to imagine the fury of the rain and lightning just a few days earlier.

As the sun began to drop in the western sky, we walked back to camp, swatting at the tiny no-seeums that seemed to be coming out with the setting sun.

Anna swatted the back of her neck, "Damn, that one hurt. These bugs are hungry tonight."

I looked to see where the bug had bitten her and could see a red welt starting to rise. Beside it, I noticed a jagged scar at the base of her head, running up into her scalp.

Back at the motorhome Anna said, "Too many bugs out here. Let's go inside and continue the party."

Inside, she opened the second bottle of wine, and I got a deck of cards out of the kitchen drawer.

She looked at the cards and laughed. "So this is how

you entertain a woman? No wonder you're still single."

I laughed, "You're right. I don't have much experience at this. Why don't you decide what we'll do."

Anna nodded, "Okay. First, we put away the cards. Then you slide over here closer to me. That way we both can see the sun set."

I did as I was told. I slid over by Anna and she pulled my arm over her shoulder.

"Now, isn't this better?" Anna asked.

"Yes, this is nice. Now what?"

Anna sighed, "Just do nothing. Enjoy the sunset. Enjoy my company. Enjoy the wine."

And that's what we did.

We talked about the day, about the treasures we'd both found, and about Jake the treasure finding wonder dog.

"Do you really believe Jake can sniff out treasure?" Anna asked.

"I don't know. But he led me right to it. He sat on the spot. Even started digging the hole."

Anna shook her head, "I'd give anything to have my own Jake the wonder dog."

"Me too. Speaking of finding treasure, are we going back out tomorrow?"

Anna nodded, "You bet. Same schedule as today. We'll get up early, then head to my secret beach. Hopefully, no one has beat us to it."

I smiled, "Sounds good. Maybe tomorrow will be as

lucky as today."

"I hope so," said Anna. "I still can't believe we found all that treasure. And I have twenty five thousand dollars in my gym bag!"

Then she asked, "What are you going to do with all the stuff you found? Are you going to take it to Ken and sell it?"

"I'm not sure. I'm thinking of holding on to it for a while. As a souvenir of our first treasure hunting adventure. If I ever need the money, I can always sell it later."

Anna nodded, then said, "Well, it's getting late. Time for me to head over to my tent. We've got an early morning tomorrow."

"Anna, please stay here tonight. The couch is a lot softer than the ground. And Bob will miss you."

She said, "Nope, I've already been over here too long. It might be dangerous if I stay. I've had too much to drink, and I'm too happy. If I stay, I might let you have your way with me."

She wagged her finger at me, "And we both know that would create problems."

She then leaned over and kissed me on the lips.

Standing she said, "Not bad. Maybe we should do that again sometime." She smiled and said, "Gotta go."

As she walked to the door I said, "Anna, I'm leaving the door unlocked and the bed set up. If you change your mind, come back over."

She waved, and walked out the door.

50

The next morning, I awoke disoriented.

Next to a warm body.

Had Anna returned during the night?

Then I heard snoring.

It was Bob. He had curled up beside me during the night.

Somewhat disappointed, I started thinking about the previous evening's celebration with Anna. It had gone well. Just wished she had stayed the night.

Then I realized I could smell bacon cooking. And I could hear noises from the kitchen. Someone was cooking breakfast. Inside the motorhome.

Pulling on my pants, I stumbled out of bed, and walked up front to find Anna in the kitchen, cracking eggs into a skillet.

She smiled, "Morning, sleepy head. Glad to see you're finally awake."

I ran a hand through my hair, "How long you been up?"

"Oh, about an hour. I couldn't sleep, and finally gave up trying. At daylight I came over here and started breakfast. Figured you might need something to eat before we headed out."

Anna pointed to an empty wine bottle on the counter, "So how's your head this morning? Got a hangover?"

I nodded, "Yes, and it's your fault." Then I asked, "Do I have time to take a quick shower before we eat?"

"Sure, as long as you don't mind eating cold eggs. Because they're ready now."

I passed on the shower. Instead, I pulled on a shirt, washed my hands, and headed to the table to eat breakfast.

As we were eating, Anna pulled a packet of Goody's Headache Powders from her shirt pocket.

"Take one of these. You'll feel better."

Downing the powder with a glass of orange juice, I had high hopes the caffeine and aspirin ingredients would soon clear the remnants of my hangover.

"So what are the plans for today?" I asked.

Anna smiled, "As soon as you get your act together, we'll head out to the beach.

"Then around one, high tide comes rolling in, so we'll come back here. Then I've got to go into town, take care of some business."

I nodded, "Sounds like you've got the day planned. Give me five minutes and I'll be ready."

I took a quick shower, shaved, and brushed my teeth. After checking Bob's food supply and refilling his water bowl, I was ready to go.

Anna was waiting for me at the door. "Walker, anybody ever tell you that you take longer than a girl to get ready?"

I smiled.

51

We put our detecting gear in the back of Anna's Land Cruiser and headed out.

As we passed the McLarty Treasure museum on A1A, we noticed several cars and trucks parked in the same place we had parked the previous morning.

Pointing at them, Anna said, "Looks like the treasure hunters are out in force today. Sure glad we were out here yesterday before it got crowded."

"Me too," I agreed, "Just wish we had Jake the wonder dog with us today. He was a lot of help yesterday."

Anna nodded, then said, "We're going to the secret beach I told you about. Hopefully, we'll be the only ones there."

After another ten minutes of driving, Anna slowed and turned left onto a short driveway blocked by a elaborate wrought iron gate.

At the gate, Anna rolled down her window and punched a few numbers on a metal keypad affixed to a pole on the left side of the drive.

The gate immediately opened, and Anna drove through, pulling into a parking space under a Key West style home built up on concrete piers.

She turned to me, "The people who own this place are away this time of the year. They won't mind if we park here."

"They're friends of yours?" I asked.

"Not really. When I was working as a meter reader for the power company, this house was on my route. The owners gave me their gate code so I could come on the grounds to read the meter.

"I checked earlier this week, and saw that they were away. So I figure they won't mind if we park here."

Anna got out and went to the back of the Cruiser and got her detecting gear and suited up. I did the same.

As she locked up the Cruiser I asked, "Are you sure it'll be okay for us to park here?"

"Yeah it's okay. I know the people. They won't be around. Don't worry about it."

She turned and walked down a paved path leading to the side of the home facing the ocean. From there, I could see that the home was built on a dune, rising about forty feet above the Atlantic. The views out over the water were incredible.

I continued to follow Anna as the path joined a wooden walkway which led to a large deck overlooking the beach.

The deck was separated from the beach by a

weathered fence with a small gate in the center, which opened to stairs leading down.

Standing on the deck, Anna scanned the beach. "Looks like we're the only ones here so far. That's good. We'll have the place to ourselves."

"We'll do like we did yesterday. We'll search in grids. You go north about 100 yards, and then turn back south. Repeat that until you cover from the dune to the waters edge."

She continued, "I'll do the same going south. If you find something big, get my attention and I'll come running."

Then she smiled, "Good luck. Hope today is as good as yesterday."

Anna opened the gate and climbed down the steps leading to the beach.

I followed.

On the beach, we turned our detectors on and started out on our grids.

It was a beautiful day. The sun was shining. The sky was blue. And the temperature was in the mid sixties. Perfect weather.

I followed my grid line going north, sticking as close to the sand dune as I could. I swung the detector coil slowly, hoping to hear the tone that would tell me that I had found something of interest.

For the first thirty yards, I found nothing. Not even a single peep from the detector.

Thinking that maybe something was wrong with the settings, I reached into my pants pocket, found a dime and dropped it on the sand.

Swinging the detector over the dime, it immediately signaled a tone indicating metal. The detector was working as it should.

Reassured, I continued my grid search.

After walking what I thought was at least one hundred yards, I turned around, moved over six feet, and started detecting a line going back the way I had just come.

I could see Anna in the distance doing the same thing. It looked like her luck today was no better than mine.

We both continued detecting along our grid lines. When I was detecting a grid facing Anna, I'd see her occasionally stop and swing the detector several times over a single location.

Then she'd either dig the spot with her scoop, or shake her head and continue on the path.

We did this for three hours, and during that time the only things I had found were four heavily encrusted iron nails.

With each pass on my grid, I moved closer to the incoming surf. I knew that when I reached the waterline, it would mean detecting this grid would be over.

After four hours and not finding anything significant, I was looking forward to moving to another location.

Finally, I reached the waterline. Still no major finds. No gold. No silver.

Anna and I met at the end point of our first grid.

I asked her, "You find anything?"

She shook her head, "No, just a few nails. What about you?"

"About the same. A few nails, some rust chips, no coins."

Anna smiled, "That's the way it goes. Some days you find treasure. But most days you don't.

"Yesterday was the best day because so much sand was stripped away. But last night's high tide brought a lot of sand back in. So treasure won't be easy to find from here on out."

"Still, being on the beach on a day like today is better than working for a living."

She was right about that. Being on the beach was a whole lot better than working in an office or a factory. Both of which I'd recently done.

Thinking about that cheered me up. What happened next would cheer me up even more.

52

"So," asked Anna, "do you want to keep detecting here, or do you want to try somewhere else?"

I thought for a moment, and then said, "Since we're already here, let's stay here. But let's go south."

Anna nodded, "Sounds good to me. But this time, let's detect in the same direction. You at the waterline and me up near the dune. That way, we'll stay close."

I agreed, and we both set out to follow the same path going south, separated by about twenty feet of beach.

Early on, I'd learned my detector would start to send false signals near the water's edge. To prevent that I had to do a ground balance on the wet sand.

I took a moment, did the ground balance, and the falsing stopped. Then I followed the edge of the incoming tide, swinging my detector slowly over the shallow water and wet sand.

Anna was slightly ahead of me up on the edge of the dune, and I was able to keep an eye on her as she swung her detector, looking for treasure.

As before, her movements were gracefully fluid. Almost like a ballet dancer.

I watched her as I slowly moved south. The headphones over my ears muted the sound of the incoming tide, and the warm sun on my back lulled me into a detecting trance.

I may have covered fifty feet, maybe more while in that lulled state. Occasionally glancing over to watch Anna's graceful progress.

A sharp tone in my ears broke the spell. I stopped and looked at the display screen on the detector. It indicated a large object buried at least twelve inches deep in the sand directly in front of me.

Grabbing my scoop, I started removing layer after layer of sand. I'd dump the sand on the beach, and run my detector over the it to see if I'd recovered the object. If there were no tone, I'd remove another layer of sand and repeat the process.

Being close to the incoming tide, the sand was wet, and keeping it from falling back into the ever increasingly deep hole was becoming a challenge.

At about fourteen inches, the scoop hit metal. Whatever it was, it was large. Much larger than a coin.

Getting down on my hands and knees, I started digging the sand out from around the object.

The more sand I cleared away, the more I could see that whatever the object was at least thirty inches long. After clearing away enough sand, I could see that the target looked a lot like a piece of iron re-bar, a common construction material.

But if it were re-bar, it was oddly shaped. It had a large lump on one end.

Glancing up, I noticed Anna walking over.

"What'd you find?", she asked.

"I don't know. But looks pretty old."

I reached under the object and carefully pulled it from the wet sand. It came up in one piece.

Brushing the sand off, I held it up so Anna could see.

She took the object from me, and after a moment she said, "I'm not sure, but this might be a Spanish rapier. It looks like this end is the handle, and the other end is the blade."

"A rapier?" I asked.

"A small sword. The Spanish sailors carried them. I saw one in the McLarty museum and it looked a lot like this."

I smiled, "A rapier, huh? Wouldn't that be cool."

She nodded, then said, "Guess what I found."

"You found something? Let me see."

Anna held up a small gold ring.

"It's a hand made ring. Looks like it was hammered out of single piece of gold. And it looks pretty old."

She held out her hand, "Go ahead and pick it up. You'll be amazed at how heavy it is."

I took the ring from her and she was right, it was a

lot heavier than I expected.

The gold shined bright. The ring wasn't damaged in any way.

I smiled as I handed the ring back to her, "That's a pretty nice ring. Where'd you find it?"

She pointed over her shoulder, "Down there. I almost missed it. The detector gave a very faint signal and I figured it was just another nail. But I dug anyway.

"And about a foot down, I found the ring. It's the only decent thing I found all day. Everything else was just rust chips."

I nodded, "Me too. Other than this, all I found was nails and rust. But I'm not complaining. I found what might be a rapier. And you found a ring, and That's pretty good.

"You want to keep detecting?" I asked.

Anna looked at her watch, "I wish we could, but the tide's coming in. This beach will be under water in less than an hour. And I need to go into town and take care of some business."

We decided to call it a day. Back at the Land Cruiser, we stowed our gear, and left through the same gate we had come in, making sure it closed behind us.

Back at the campsite, Bob met us at the door, and soon was purring while rubbing his head against Anna's ankle.

"Bob sure likes you," I said. "He starts purring as soon as he sees you."

Anna smiled, "Maybe if you'd treat him better, he'd like you too."

I laughed, "I treat Bob like a king. And he repays me by loving up on you, right in front of me."

Anna smiled, "That's because he's got good taste in women."

Then she hugged me, grabbed her gym bag and said, "I've got to run. I should be back in a few hours."

"You want me to go with you?"

"No, I need to take care of this on my own. But I'll be back later. And if you want, I can pick up some food and we can have dinner together."

"Sounds good. Call me if anything comes up."

We exchanged phone numbers. Anna kissed me on the cheek on her way out the door.

53

While Anna was gone, I took the opportunity to clean up the motorhome. I'd been at the campsite for five days and trash and dirty clothes had been piling up.

I stuffed the clothes into a pillow case, grabbed a handful of quarters, and walked to the campground restrooms where they had laundry facilities.

I started two loads of clothes, and then headed back to the motorhome. Inside, I swept up the sand we'd tracked in from the beach, cleaned Bob's litter box, and emptied all the trash cans.

Remembering my clothes, I walked back to the laundry room, and moved the clothes from the washing machines into dryers.

Forty minutes later, my clothes were dry and I took them back to the motorhome and hung them in the bedroom closet.

Since Anna had yet to return, I retrieved my laptop from its hiding place in the bedroom, and checked my email.

Nothing important and no messages from Sarah.

After checking the email, I decided to search Google for 'Spanish rapiers' to see if anyone else had found one.

It didn't take long to discover that at least three had been found on the Treasure Coast, and the photos looked very similar to the one I had found.

All were heavily encrusted, but the general shape and size were the same.

Surprisingly, while the rapiers were quite rare, they were not exceptionally valuable. They didn't contain any gold or silver, and were only sought out as museum curiosities.

The most recent one that sold at auction had fetched just under one thousand dollars.

On the same auction site, I saw a ring similar to the one Anna had found, and it had sold for more than five thousand dollars. Good for Anna.

Looking further, I found a ring similar to the one I had found, hammered gold with a big green emerald.

I was astounded to see that it had an asking price of more than four hundred thousand dollars!

That meant that the combined value of the gold and silver coins I had found, along with the ring would be a lot. Probably a lot more than a hundred thousand dollars!

Not bad for two days walking on the beach.

As I was thinking about this, a knock on the door

brought me back to earth.

"Walker, it's me. Come out here. I got something to show you."

It was Anna. She had returned from her trip into town.

Opening the door, Anna stood there grinning from ear to ear.

"Guess what I bought!"

placed below the entry, and stepped in.

The inside was bright and clean, with smooth white walls, white kitchen counter and cabinets, and white trimmed windows.

At the far end of the trailer was a dinette table that presumably folded into a bed. At the near end was a small bathroom with toilet and shower.

In the center, a kitchen on the same side as the entry door, and across from that was small table with two seats.

Anna stepped in behind me, "Isn't this cool? Everything a person needs."

I could tell she was proud of her new home on wheels.

"Anna this is great. I would have never guessed it would be so nice inside. Is this new?"

"No, it just looks new. It's actually ten years old. But the previous owner really took good care of it."

Anna took a breath and continued, "I was driving through Vero today and saw this on an RV lot. I pulled in expecting the price to be way too high.

"But the dealer made me an offer I couldn't pass up. You'll never guess what I paid for it."

Anna paused, waiting for me to guess the price.

Thinking about what I'd seen similar trailers sell for, I said, "I'd be surprised if it was under ten thousand dollars."

Anna nodded in agreement. "That's what I was

thinking. But when the dealer said I could have it for fifty five hundred, I couldn't resist.

"That price included electric brakes, a full tank of propane, and a thirty day warranty."

I nodded, "That is an amazing price. It looks like you got a great deal.

"So how well does it tow behind the Cruiser?"

Anna smiled, "It's tows beautifully. In fact, other than it blocking my rear view mirror, you can't really tell it's there going down the road."

I put my hand on her shoulder, "Anna, you did good. I'm really happy for you."

She nodded, then pointed at the dinette, "Sit down. We need to talk."

Uh-oh. I knew this couldn't be good. Whenever a woman tells you she needs to talk, it almost never ends well.

I sat and waited for the bad news.

55

"Walker, I've been keeping some things from you. I wanted to tell you earlier, but I just didn't find the right time.

"Well, now's the time.

"First of all, you never asked my last name, and I never told you. My full name is Anna Parker."

She paused, waiting for me to say something.

"Okay," I said, "So your name is Anna Parker. Is that supposed to mean something to me?"

She frowned, "How long have you been in Florida?"

"Three months. Why?"

"That explains it. You weren't here when it happened.

"See, six months ago while I was reading meters on my route, I was assaulted.

"I was out on foot, walking between homes, reading meters. A man walked up behind me and hit me in the head with an iron pipe. "

She pointed to the scar on the back of her head.

"I was knocked unconscious. When I woke up, I was on the ground, my shirt had been ripped off, and this guy was standing over me with a knife.

"He sat down on my legs and when he did, I reached for my belly pack. I pulled out my gun and shot him. Twice.

"He fell on top of me and I blacked out. I woke up in the hospital three days later. They told me the guy was dead.

Anna looked away, then continued. "A neighbor's security camera caught the whole thing. They gave the video to the sheriff, and he said it was a clear case of self defense. They didn't charge me.

"But they released the video of the attack to the media. And the news stations ran it over and over and over. They called me Anna 'get your gun' Parker.

"The video of the attack made headlines all over Florida, and it wasn't long before politicians used me as an example of why the state needed tougher laws.

When she paused, I said, "Anna, you don't have to tell me this."

Shaking her head, she said, "No, you should know."

She continued, "Since I was on duty when it happened, the power company covered all my medical expenses. They continued to pay me during my recovery.

"But then the family of the man I shot sued the company. Said it was their fault I had a gun. They said the guy would still be alive if the company hadn't allowed me to carry a gun on duty.

"The judge threw the case out. But after that, the power company decided it couldn't set a precedent by allowing an employee to get away with carrying a gun. So they quietly let me go.

"They gave me a good severance package, and that's what I've been living on ever since.

"Because of the video, just about everyone in Florida recognizes my name or face.

"And I should have told you about this earlier."

A few moments passed in silence, then I said, "Anna, I'm sorry you were attacked. But I'm glad you were able to defend yourself."

She smiled. "There's one more thing I need to tell you. And you might not like this.

"You know that first day, when I picked you up in the rain?"

I nodded.

"Well . . ."

Before Anna could finish, someone knocked at the door.

56

Anna opened the door to an older man. He was holding a printed page with a photo on it.

The man looked familiar, but I didn't immediately recognize him.

"Hope I'm not disturbing you folks. But my dog is lost, and I'm visiting everyone here in the park checking to see if they've seen him."

He handed Anna the sheet of paper he'd been holding, and it had a photo of a black lab. Below the photo was one word, "Jake".

I looked at the man and said, "Jake's missing?"

The man looked at me closely, and I could see the recognition in his eyes.

"You're the ones who pulled my car out of the sand on Monday. And I saw you on the beach Tuesday."

"Yes, that's right. And Jake was with you on Tuesday."

The man nodded, "Yes, that's the day he went missing.

"See, when the tide came in, we went back to our car in the Sebastian Beach lot. I went to the restroom and Jake stayed outside. When I came back out, he was gone.

"I thought he had run back to the beach, so I went and looked for him. But couldn't find him.

"I figured he'd eventually come back to the car, so I stayed and waited for him.

"I waited until they ran me out of the park when they closed the gates at dark, and still no Jake."

"I drove up and down the beach road until midnight, and still didn't find him.

"I finally went home, and this morning I made up these fliers with his picture and went back to the beach looking for him.

"Jake has never run off before. He sticks with me. So the only thing I could figure was maybe someone over here at the campground got him.

"Maybe they thought they were rescuing a lost dog."

He paused, then said, "So, have you seen him over here?"

Anna and I both shook our heads.

I spoke first. "The last time I saw Jake was when he ran up to you on the beach Tuesday. Have you called Animal Control? Maybe they picked him up."

"Yes, I called Animal Control. They said no."

I could tell the man was distraught. His Jake was missing.

I introduced myself, "I'm Walker and this is Anna. And if you want, I'll help you find Jake."

"Me too," Anna chimed in.

The man brightened, "I'm Walt. And I would appreciate any help I can get finding Jake."

He pulled a map of the island out of his pocket.

"I've been searching around the beach parking lot because that's the last place I saw him. From there, I hiked down to the McLarty museum, and still no Jake.

"My plan now is to to talk to everyone here in the campground, then go back to the beach and look some more."

As I looked at the map, I could see there were eight miles of beach that Walt had yet to cover.

I pointed to the map, "I can cover the beach from the museum down to Treasure Shores park. "

Anna nodded, "I'll cover the other side of the road in the same area. Let's exchange phone numbers so that if we find him, we can let each other know."

We exchanged numbers, and Walt reached for the door. Before stepping out he said, "I'm offering a five thousand dollar reward if you find him."

I shook my head, "I'm not interested in the reward. I just want to see you reunited with Jake."

With a pained smile, Walt said, "Call me if you find him." Then he left the trailer.

I turned to Anna, "Jake the wonder dog is missing. We've got to find him."

She nodded, "Yes, we do. Let's get started."

57

We still had at least three hours of daylight, so we decided to immediately begin our search for Jake.

Anna drove to the McLarty museum and dropped me off. Her plan was to drive the back roads on the Indian River side of the island, while I hiked the dunes south of the museum.

We'd detected in this area the day before, and it was the last place I'd seen Jake. So starting here and going south, I hoped that he'd somehow returned to this area and gotten lost.

I began hiking south, staying on the road side of the dune, while staying off the sea oats which were protected by Florida state law.

I eventually found and followed a trail up over the dunes, used by other travelers and perhaps even by Jake.

Slogging through the soft sand on the dry side of the dune was hard going, but being higher up allowed me a better view of the area.

The search was frustrating. There were no signs of Jake, just signs of beer parties thrown by late night revelers.

After an hour of searching, I checked in with Anna. She answered on the third ring.

"You find him?" she asked.

"No, nothing over here. How you doing on your side?"

"Not good. Nothing over here except a lot of muddy roads."

I could hear the discouragement in her voice.

"Let's keep searching until dark. Call me if you find anything." I hung up.

Continuing my search, I began to run out of public beach and encountering private homes behind walls and gates. The only way around these was to get back on the road and walk the shoulder.

My phone chimed. It was Anna.

"Walker, it's getting dark. Time to call off the search. I'm heading out to A1A. Be on the road so I can pick you up."

A few minutes later, Anna pulled up in her Land Cruiser, which was now splattered with a layer of milky mud.

I got in and she shook her head, "No Jake. But maybe Walt had better luck."

I called, and he had struck out as well. No luck in finding Jake.

We all agreed it was too dangerous to hike the dunes or the highway at night, and that we'd resume our search in the morning.

Back at camp, Anna was subdued. I could tell something was bothering her.

"Anna, what's up?"

"Just bummed out about Jake. I thought we'd be celebrating my new trailer tonight. But with Jake missing, I feel bad for Walt."

I nodded, then said, "I've got an idea. Let's invite Walt over for dinner. He can tell us more about Jake and we can work out plans for tomorrow's search."

Anna smiled, "That's a good idea. You call him while I go look through your freezer for something to cook for dinner."

I called Walt and invited him over to eat with us. I explained that we wanted to find out more about where Jake could be, as well as work out plans for tomorrow's search.

Walt accepted our invite, and said he'd be right over.

Anna returned from my motorhome, her arms filled with food and plates. She said, "I'm going to cook in my new trailer. Hope you don't mind."

I didn't.

Thirty minutes later, Walt pulled in behind Anna's Land Cruiser.

We were standing outside Anna's trailer, and she spoke first, "Glad you were able to make it. Hope you like salmon."

He nodded, "Salmon sounds great." Then he walked

up to Anna's trailer, and ran his hand over the exterior.

"Is this fiberglass?"

Anna said, "Yes it is. Isn't it cute?"

"That it is," said Walt. "It's a nice looking rig. But is there room for both of you inside?"

Anna laughed, "Walker has his own motorhome over there. It's just me in the trailer."

Walt seemed embarrassed, "My mistake. I just assumed you two were together."

"No problem," said Anna. "Walker tells me he's already got a girlfriend, so I didn't stand a chance."

They both looked at me, expecting a reply.

I had nothing to say, so I just shrugged.

Anna sat down at the picnic table, and we joined her. Looking at Walt, she said, "Tell us about Jake."

He said, "Okay, but stop me if I get long winded. I tend to do that sometimes.

"My wife had just died from cancer, and I was living alone. Three days after her funeral, I walked out to my mailbox, and on the way back, I heard a puppy crying.

"My place is overgrown, a few acres, just down the road from here. People sometimes dump their pets there.

"Anyway, I go to look, and I see this little black puppy huddled under palmetto bushes. He looked pretty sad. Hungry and dehydrated.

"I coaxed him out, brought him up to the house, and nursed him back to health.

"He's been with me ever since."

Anna smiled, "Sounds like you saved his life."

"Yeah, well, maybe I did. But he saved my life too. I was wasting away, just waiting to die. But after finding Jake, I had someone to take care of.

"He'd make me take him for walks two or three times a day, and the more we walked, the better I felt.

"We soon expanded our walks onto the beach, and that's when I discovered Jake's hidden talent.

"We were walking south of the treasure museum, and Jake started digging a hole in the sand.

"I figured he was chasing a hermit crab or something, so I didn't take any notice.

"But as I walked away, Jake stayed on top of his hole. Even when I called him, he wouldn't come. He just sat by that hole, with his paws hanging over the edge.

"I eventually walked back to get him, and that's when I discovered what was in the hole.

"Turned out to be a small gold cross. Old. Probably from the treasure fleet that sunk out there.

"I thought it was a fluke. But two months later, he did it again. That time it was a gold coin.

"Then a few months later, he found something else. And by then, I realized his special talent was finding old things buried in the sand.

"Over the years we've found lots of things. Some valuable, some not.

"I've given most of the items to the treasure

239

museum."

Walt shook his head, "I sure miss that dog. I know he's out there somewhere."

I nodded, "We'll find him tomorrow. I'm sure of it."

A small bell rang from within Anna's trailer. She rose and said, "Dinner's ready. You two sit out here and I'll get it. Walker, open some wine and pour us a glass."

58

Dinner was excellent. Anna had prepared another great meal, and Walt and I both complimented her on her ability.

After our meal, Walt thanked us for our hospitality, and said he needed to get back home so he could get a good night's sleep before resuming the search for Jake.

We agreed to stay in touch and alert him should we find Jake. He went to his car and brought back a stack of fliers with Jake's photo. Then he drove away.

After he left, Anna and I finished off the bottle of wine and talked about the stories Walt had told about Jake's ability to find treasure.

"So," I asked, "do you think it's possible that someone else knows about Jake's ability? Maybe they took him?"

Anna shook her head, "I hope not. If they've taken him off this island, we may never find him."

We were silent for a few moments. Then Anna changed the subject, "I'm sleeping over here tonight. I want to test out the bed in this camper."

I nodded, "You really got a great deal on this thing. I guess you were at the right place at the right time."

Anna smiled, then said, "Walker, has anyone ever told you that you might be a good luck charm?"

I laughed.

Anna continued, "I'm not kidding. Ever since I met you, my luck has changed. Good things have been happening. I found gold. Two days in a row.

"And then I got paid twenty five thousand dollars for the gold. And then I found this amazing deal on this camper.

"I'm thinking you're my lucky charm."

I'd heard it before. First from Sarah. Then from the fisherman on the pier. And now from Anna.

Hopefully my luck would rub off on Walt. And we'd find Jake the wonder dog tomorrow.

In the background I could hear Bob. He was starting to meow loudly. He either wanted dinner or just wanted to be reassured that someone still loved him.

Anna looked at me, "Sounds like Bob needs some attention. And it's getting late. Time for you to go take care of him."

She continued, "I've already gotten my things out of your motorhome, so I'm pretty much set for the evening. I'll bang on your door in the morning when I'm ready to search for Jake."

As I stood up to go, Anna pulled me toward her and gave me a long kiss. Then she tapped me on the chest and said, "Go home. Sleep well."

And I did.

59

Back in my motorhome, Bob met me at the door. He was in a talkative mood. Telling me something important.

I followed him as he led me back to the bathroom. His food bowl was almost empty. He didn't like that one bit.

I rubbed his head and poured some of his favorite dry food. He walked over, sniffed it, and apparently satisfied, trotted away.

My laptop was still out from earlier in the day. I connected to the internet and checked my email. No messages from Sarah.

I checked the Vero Beach Craigslist to see if anyone had posted a message about finding a lost dog. There were two recent posts, but neither dog matched Jake's description.

I remembered what Anna had told me earlier. About her being attacked. I did a Google search on her name, and quickly found hundreds of links to the story.

It was just as Anna had said. The assailant had been

killed, and Anna was hailed as a hero.

The video of her attack was available as well. I chose not to view it. Anna had already told me the story, and I wasn't interested in invading her privacy.

I now fully understood why Anna carried the gun she had shown me the first night she slept on my couch.

I hoped she would never need to use the gun again. Once in a lifetime is more than enough.

I powered down the computer and returned it to it's hiding spot in my bedroom. While in there I raised the mattress platform and checked to make sure my treasure finds were still there.

They were. I added the rapier to the collection, then lowered the bed platform, and locked it.

That night I had a strange dream.

In the dream, I was working for a large company and had been called in to do a presentation before the board of directors.

During my presentation, I showed evidence that one of the directors had embezzled millions of dollars from the company.

The directors listened intently and then after my presentation, one of them spoke up.

He said, "I think we can all see what the problem is. It's you. You're fired."

In my dream, I was upset that I had lost my job. I'd soon be homeless, with no way to support myself.

When I woke from the dream I was still worried about finding a job. About finding a place to live.

Then I remembered I didn't have a job to lose. Hadn't had one for several months. And because I had a bit of money in the bank, I didn't need to look for a job any time soon.

But I was technically homeless. I didn't have a permanent address. My home had been my motorhome parked in the boatyard next to Sarah's office. And there was a good chance that I'd soon be asked to leave.

As I lay in bed thinking about this dream, I decided I needed to do something about getting a permanent base.

I couldn't realistically expect to live in Sarah's backyard forever.

The simple solution would be to buy a small home. Something with enough room to park the motorhome. Maybe even room enough for two or three motorhomes in case friends visited.

That's what I'd do. As soon as I got back to Englewood, I'd start looking for a place of my own.

This decision gave me peace and allowed me to soon drift back to sleep. A sleep with no more unpleasant dreams.

60

It was Thursday, my sixth day camping at the Sebastian Inlet State Park on the Treasure Coast of Florida.

And today, rather than search for treasure, I'd be searching for Jake, the wonder dog.

He had been missing for two long days, and his guardian, Walt, was fearing the worst. Either Jake had been stolen or he had been mortally wounded by a careless driver.

I was optimistic. My feeling was that Jake had gotten himself trapped somewhere and couldn't get out, and he was waiting for someone to rescue him.

I was hoping that either Walt, Anna or I would find Jake today.

Knowing that the early morning low tide would make it easier for me to cover the part of the beach I couldn't get to yesterday, I got up at daybreak, ate breakfast and prepared for the hunt.

Anna had spent the night in her new camping trailer, and I had yet to hear from her this morning.

Since I was anxious to start our search for Jake, I locked up my motorhome and walked next door to Anna's campsite.

I could see from the light in her windows that she was up, so I knocked on her door.

From inside I heard, "Give me a minute, I'll be right there."

A moment later, Anna opened the door just slightly. She was wearing boxer shorts, white with red stripes, and a sleeveless t-shirt. No bra.

She had a toothbrush in one hand. "You're a little early. But since you're here, come on in."

"No thanks," I said, "I think I'll just wait out here."

"Okay, have it your way. I'll be out in a minute."

True to her word, a few minutes later she was ready. This time, fully dressed. a map in one hand, and a yellow highlighter in the other.

She put the map on the picnic table and said, "The part I've highlighted in yellow is what we covered yesterday.

"I'm thinking today you should continue down the beach and try to check out those houses that have fenced yards."

I nodded.

"While you are doing that, I'll go into town and check the Humane Society and the two other animal shelters.

"Someone may have picked up Jake and dropped

him off. I want to be sure we don't miss him.

"After I check those places, I'll come back on the island and meet up with you."

I nodded, "Sounds like a plan. Be sure to keep your cellphone nearby in case I find something."

"Will do. I'll call Walt and let him know what we're doing."

Anna looked at her watch.

"It's almost seven now, so we need to get going."

We climbed into Anna's Land Cruiser and headed out. Going south on A1A, we kept a sharp lookout for any sign of Jake.

We didn't find him and were relieved we didn't see any animal carcasses on the side of the road.

About a mile beyond the McLarty Treasure Museum, Anna slowed, then pulled over to the shoulder and stopped.

"Here's where I picked you up last night. Good luck."

I opened the door, grabbed a bottle of water, stuffed one of the fliers with Jake's photo into my pocket and got out.

61

This time of year, most of the houses on the beach are occupied by either snowbirds or seasonal renters.

Many of these people would be wary of strangers who hopped over their privacy fences or climbed their locked security gates. That meant I needed to go to each home, ring the bell at the gate, and hope someone would respond.

I'd then explain what I was doing, and ask if they had seen or heard of a dog that looked like Jake.

On homes where no one answered, I'd have to figure out a way to search the property without getting shot.

At the first home, the owners answered after I pressed the entry gate buzzer. I explained what I was doing, and they said they hadn't seen or heard a stray dog. But they would call me if one came around.

I got the same story at the next three homes. No one had seen a stray dog.

At the fifth house, there was no answer when I rang the bell at the gate. The property was surrounded by an eight foot concrete wall, and I wasn't able to see inside.

The driveway leading to the gate didn't show any signs of recent traffic, so my guess was no one was home.

Not wanting to leave the place unchecked, I walked the full length of the street side wall until it ended at a heavily overgrown vacant lot.

I could see that the vacant lot rose up onto a dune, and from up there I would be able to look down into the yard of the walled property.

I made my way through the vegetation on the vacant lot, and as I expected, from the high point I could look down onto the property beside it.

There were no signs of life. No car, nor any lights on inside the large house. It looked vacant.

I couldn't see all the way around the house though. The far side of the yard was blocked by the house itself.

Surveying the property, I could see that like most beach homes in this area, it had a deck overlooking the ocean, with steps leading down to the beach.

If I got down on the beach, and then climbed the steps, I could hop the fence around the deck and gain access to the yard.

That was my plan.

As I was approaching the steps from the beach, my phone chimed. It was Anna.

"Walker. I've checked all three shelters, and no Jake. I left fliers at each one, and asked them to call if anyone brings him in.

"I've got one more place to check, then I'm coming back to the island. How's it going with you? Find anything?"

"Nothing so far. I've checked four places and I'm about to check the next one now. No one has seen a stray dog."

Anna sighed. "We'll find him. Call me if anything comes up." She ended the call.

I put the phone back in my pocket and headed toward the steps leading up to the vacant home.

From the beach, the house still looked empty. No lights. No open windows.

I climbed the steps up to the deck, and stopped. So far, so good.

From the top of the steps, I turned toward the beach to see if anyone might be watching me.

The view out over the Atlantic ocean was spectacular. The water was deep blue, with an occasional white top. Sea birds roamed the beach, pecking at the crustaceans that rolled in with each wave.

With a view like this, it was easy to see why so many people fell in love with this side of Florida.

Fortunately, there was no one on the beach this time of the day. That was good. No witnesses to see what I was going to do next.

I hopped over the wooden fence that surrounded the deck, and quickly made my way into the yard of the home.

Since I'd already checked the south side from the adjacent lot, my plan was to walk around the north side. If I didn't find Jake there, I'd leave the way I came in.

A stone walkway led to the base of the home. From there, the walkway went both north and south.

Following the walkway north, I came to the edge of the home, and at that point I noticed a well tended vegetable garden.

This was my first indication that someone was either living here, or visiting regularly to tend the garden.

As I got closer to the garden, I could see a large hole dug out of the center. Muddy paw prints led away toward one of the doors under the house.

Was it possible that these paw prints were left by Jake?

Looking around and not seeing any sign of him, I called out his name.

"Jake!"

Almost immediately, I heard a muffled bark.

I called his name again, and again heard a muffled bark.

The bark sounded like it was coming from within the home.

Walking over to a ground floor window, I peered in. A curtain blocked my view.

While squinting through the glass, I heard the very distinctive sound of the hammer being cocked on a revolver.

A woman's voice behind me said, "Hands in the air!"

62

"Now, turn around slowly. No funny stuff."

As I turned around, hands above my head, I saw a woman holding a gun.

About five foot four, maybe ninety pounds, silver hair. Probably in her late sixties.

In her right hand she held a black six shot revolver. Pointed directly at me.

She said, "So tell me why I shouldn't shoot you."

"Ma'am," I replied, "I'm looking for a lost dog. I think he might be in your basement."

I reached for my shirt pocket.

"Sonny, unless you want a new hole in that shirt, put your hands back up over your head."

"Yes, ma'am."

"So, tell me more about this dog you're looking for."

With my hands still over my head, I answered, "It's a big black Labrador. And he's bad about digging holes in the dirt. Maybe he dug the one in your garden over there?"

The lady with the gun looked at the garden then back at me.

"Let's say I might know something about that dog. And maybe he did dig up my garden. Who's going to replant my tomatoes?"

"Ma'am, I'll be happy to fill in that hole and replant your tomatoes. Even if you don't have the dog, I'll be glad to do that."

She nodded, then said. "I'll tell you what. You fill in the hole and plant the tomatoes first. Then we'll talk about the dog. How does that sound?"

"That's fine with me. Just one condition. You quit pointing that gun at me."

"No, can't do that. As soon as I put this gun down, you could jump me. Or run off and not fill in the hole that dog dug."

I smiled, "How about this? I call a friend and she'll pick up some tomato plants from town.

"Then she and I will replant your garden, and then you can release Jake."

The woman shook the gun, "Who's Jake?"

"Jake is the dog. I've got his photo in my shirt pocket."

The woman shifted her gaze toward my pocket, then said, "Okay, here's what I want you to do.

"With your right hand, slowly reach into your shirt pocket and get the photo. Then bring it over here and place it on the picnic table. Then stand back. And no sudden moves."

I did as instructed.

The woman picked up the flier and looked at it carefully.

"Looks like you're telling the truth about the dog. That's one thing in your favor.

"Who's the friend you're going to call about the plants? What's her name?"

"Anna. Anna Parker."

"She your wife? Girlfriend?"

I shook my head, "Neither. Anna's just a good friend."

The woman rubbed her chin with her free hand and said, "Anna Parker? Why does that name sound so familiar?"

Oops. Anna had told me that a lot of people around Vero Beach would recognize her name. And that might include the woman holding a gun on me.

The woman brightened, "I remember now. Anna Parker is the girl who shot that guy last year. Is your Anna related to her?"

"Yes ma'am. My Anna is the one who did that."

She put the gun down, "Why didn't you say so in the first place? That girl is my hero. I want to meet her. Call her. Tell her to come over, right now.

"And be sure to tell her to bring six tomato plants. Three romas and three cherries."

I reached into my pocket and slowly retrieved my

phone and called Anna.

"Anna, I've found Jake. He's safe. But he dug up a garden, and we need to replace some tomato plants. Are you still on the mainland?"

"Yes," she replied. "Just getting to the bridge now."

"Good, before you come back, stop and pick up six tomato plants. Three romas, and three cherries.

"Get the biggest, nicest ones you can find. Then come back on the island. I'm at the fifth house down from the treasure museum. Ring the bell at the gate when you get here."

"Walker, is everything okay?"

"Yep, everything is fine. Just find some tomato plants and get over here as quick as you can."

We ended the call.

The lady pointed at my phone, "Was that really Anna Parker? Is she really coming over here?"

"Yes ma'am, that was Anna, and yes, she's coming over here."

The lady smiled brightly, "I've got to go inside and get ready. I can't let her see me like this. She's famous."

Then she said, "I'm going to trust that you won't run off when I go in. You'll stay here, right?"

"Yes ma'am. I'll stay right here."

"You do that." She turned and went inside.

After a few moments I picked up my phone and called Walt.

No answer, so I left a message, "Walt, we found Jake. He's safe. I'll call back later with details."

Then I called Anna again.

"Anna, couldn't talk earlier. But here's the deal. Jake's safe. The woman who has him wants us to replant the tomatoes Jake dug up in her garden. That's why we need the plants. How long before you get here?"

"I'm paying for the plants right now. I should be there in about fifteen minutes."

"Good. I'll be waiting for you."

63

I was waiting outside the house. Alone. And thinking about the hole Jake had dug.

The last time he had dug a hole, we found treasure in it. Gold and silver. And Walt said this was Jake's secret talent. Finding treasure.

Was that why Jake dug up the garden? Had he found treasure again?

My thoughts were interrupted by the sound of the sliding glass door behind me.

The woman no longer held a gun. She had changed clothes, combed her hair. Applied some makeup. She looked nice.

Looking at me, she said. "So, you didn't leave."

"No ma'am, I'm still here.'

She held out her hand, "Please don't call me ma'am. My name is Frances Ford. Just call me Frances."

I shook her hand gently, "I'm Walker. Glad to meet you, Frances. And I'm real sorry about what Jake did. We'll clean it up."

"So is Jake your dog?"

"No ma'am, I mean Frances.

"Jake belongs to Walt, a man we met on the beach a few days ago. He's had Jake since he was a pup, and he's worried sick that he might lose him."

Frances nodded and said, "I once had a dog that looked a whole lot like Jake. He was my best friend and companion for years. Eventually old age got to him."

I nodded.

She continued, "Jake looks so much like the one I had. I wonder if they might be related?"

"Might be," I replied. "Walt said that someone abandoned Jake as a pup on his property about six years ago. He lives a few miles up the road from here, so who knows, the two dogs might be related."

Frances nodded, then said, "Tell me what you know about this Walt. Is he single?"

I nodded, "Yes, ma'am, Walt is single. He told us his wife passed several years back, and it's just been him and Jake ever since.

"He's about your age, and he seems like a decent sort of guy. I imagine he'll be thrilled and thankful that you rescued his Jake."

Frances smiled, "I'd like to meet this Walt."

I nodded, "I think I can arrange that."

I pulled out my phone and called him. This time he answered. I told him Jake was safe, and I gave him directions to Frances Ford's home. Asked him to come over as soon as he could.

Ten minutes later, the driveway bell announced Anna's arrival at the gate. Frances brightened and asked me, "How do I look?"

"You look great."

Frances pressed the gate unlock button and Anna drove in. I walked around the house and met her as she was getting out of the Cruiser.

She pointed to the rear, "Tomato plants are in the back."

I walked around, opened the hatch, and grabbed the flat which contained six very healthy tomato plants.

"Follow me," I said to Anna, "there's someone I want you to meet."

When we came around the corner, Frances was waiting for us.

"Anna, this is Frances Ford."

"Frances, this is Anna Parker."

Anna looked at me and frowned, reminding me she wasn't comfortable letting people know her last name.

Frances said, "Anna, I'm so excited to meet you. You're my hero."

Anna blushed, "I'm pretty sure I'm not a hero."

Frances continued, "Oh, but you are. So many women look up to you. You did exactly what should of been done."

Then she said, "Come up here and let's talk. We can watch while Walker plants the tomatoes."

Anna stepped up onto the deck with Frances, then nodded toward me, "Walker, you need to go back to the car and get the digging tools.

"And bring the metal detector."

"Why's he need a metal detector?" asked Frances.

Anna smiled, "There might be water or power lines under the garden. He can use the detector to make sure he doesn't accidentally dig them up."

I knew this wasn't the real reason Anna wanted me to get the detector. She too wanted to see what led Jake to the hole he had dug.

64

Frances Ford and Anna stood on the wooden deck above me as I began the work in the garden.

The hole that Jake had dug was about three feet wide and two feet deep. Dirt from the hole was piled on just one side, indicating Jake had dug with his front paws, kicking the dirt up behind him.

Before I filled the hole back in, I was determined to use my detector to see if Jake had sensed something in the ground where he'd dug.

Swinging the detector in the bottom of the hole, it immediately produced a low volume beep, indicating a metal object below.

Using the sand scoop, I dug down six inches and dumped the dirt outside the hole. I checked the newly removed dirt with the detector. Nothing.

This meant the object was still in the hole. To confirm this, I put the detector back in, and again got a tone. This time much stronger.

The display screen on the detector indicated an object not much larger than a nickle, about four inches below the bottom of the hole.

Placing the detector aside, I got down on my knees and started removing dirt one handful at a time.

On the third try, I felt something solid.

I retrieved the object, then turned to Anna and Frances and said, "Look what I found. A ring."

I stood, walked over to the deck, and handed the ring to Anna, then went back to the hole to see if there was anything else in it.

This time, swinging the detector resulted in no tones. I repeated the swing several times, with the same results. Nothing there.

Leaving the hole, I swung the detector through the entire garden plot, being careful not to disturb the remaining plants.

No tones. The ring was the only target to be found.

From behind me, I heard crying.

I turned to see Frances Ford softly sobbing. Anna was comforting the older woman, an arm around her shoulders.

Anna looked at me and held a finger to her mouth, the universal sign to keep quiet. Honoring her request, I said nothing as I walked closer.

Frances Ford was holding the ring in her hand and smiling through her tears.

Anna explained, "It's her Grandmother's wedding ring. Frances had worn that ring for almost fifty years. Then one day she noticed it was gone. She searched for it for months without any luck. She thought it was gone forever.

"And today, you found it."

Frances beckoned me toward her and said, "I owe you an apology. I should have never held that gun on you. Instead I should be giving you a reward. You found my ring."

I smiled, "I didn't find your ring. Jake did. He's special that way.

"Speaking of Jake, can we let him out now? I think he's earned his freedom."

Frances pointed to the basement door. "It's unlocked, just open the door and he'll come out."

I did, and Jake bounded out. He ran directly to Frances and stopped in front of her and sat.

Then he ran to the hole in the garden, inspected it, and then returned to sit in front of Frances.

I smiled, "He looks healthy. And he seems to like you Frances."

She nodded, "I've been taking good care of him. Feeding him, giving him water. I even read him a story last night when he started crying."

The bell on the gate announced the arrival of Walt. Jake seemed to know who it was. He stood, wagging his tail, waiting in anticipation.

Frances pressed the button that opened the gate, and I walked around to meet Walt and tell him the story.

"Jake was rescued by this very nice lady. She and you

have a lot in common, and you should take a few minutes to talk with her before you leave with Jake."

I led Walt around to the deck where Anna and Frances were seated. Jake jumped up and ran to him, tail swinging wildly.

Walt bent down and hugged Jake, and it was obvious they had missed each other immensely.

After Jake settled down, Walt went over and spoke with Frances. She invited him to sit for a moment, and then went inside to get iced tea for all of us.

After taking a sip of tea, I resumed my task of planting the new tomato plants while Anna, Frances, and Walt watched and gave me advice.

A half hour later, the plants were in the ground and watered to everyone's satisfaction. Frances and Walt were still talking about their lives and loves and they seemed to be hitting it off quite well.

Anna stood and walked over to me.

"Walker, you've done it again. Good things happen to people around you. You are like a lucky charm or something."

I shook my head, "No, it wasn't me this time. It was Jake."

Anna smiled, "That might be true, but it was you who found Jake. It was you who found the ring. And it was you who put Walt and Francis together.

"Their meeting like this might be the luckiest thing that ever happened to both of them."

Anna walked over to Frances and said that if she was satisfied with my planting job, we needed to get going.

Frances offered to pay us a reward for finding her ring. And Walt said we earned the reward he was offering for the return of Jake.

Without hesitation, Anna said, "We don't want a reward. Keep it. Or donate it to the local animal shelters. They need it more than we do."

Frances then whispered something in Anna's ear. They both laughed, then looked at me.

Anna shook her head, blushed and walked over to me. "Time to go."

We waved to Frances and Walt as we got into the Cruiser and drove away.

65

As we headed south on A1A, Anna turned and handed me a small card.

"What's this?"

"It's from Frances. It's her business card.

"While you were planting the tomatoes, she and I had a long talk. Apparently, she is very well off.

"Her family owns several luxury hotels in south Florida, and she is the major share holder in the company.

"She said if you ever needed a place to stay, or a a job, or anything else, call her."

I took the card and looked at it. Printed neatly in the center was 'Frances Ford.'

At the bottom right corner was her phone number, and underneath that, her email address.

"Nice of her to make the offer. I'll keep the card. Never know when it might come it handy.

"So what else did you and Frances Ford talk about? And what was that she whispered to you when you were leaving? When you both looked at me and giggled."

Anna reached over and touched my arm, "Walker, that was just girl talk. Nothing for you to worry about.

"And just in case you wondered, Frances Ford thinks you're a hottie. Says if she were a few years younger, she might have tried to hook up with you."

I laughed, "She said that? Hook up? What's the world coming to?"

Anna laughed, "Frances was really happy about what you did for her. Finding that ring is something she won't forget.

"And look what you did for Walt. You found his beloved Jake. That means you did at least two good deeds today."

I nodded, and then said, "You helped. Don't forget that. Frances Ford was about to shoot me until I mentioned your name. You're like a celebrity to her.

"Do you get that reaction a lot?"

Anna nodded, "Sometimes it works out that way. Sometimes not. Personally I'd prefer people just forget about the whole thing."

We rode in silence for a few moments, then I asked, "Where are we going? The campground is the other way."

"Yeah, I know. I just thought that since it was so late, you might want to grab lunch at the Vero Island Deli. "

I nodded, "Sounds good to me."

66

It was after two when we arrived at the Deli. There wasn't a crowd, so we didn't have to wait. Anna ordered our sandwiches to go and I paid.

Ten minutes later, our order was ready and Anna drove us to the nearby Jaycee Park where we found a table under the trees.

As we ate our sandwiches, Anna said, "You mentioned earlier that you planned to leave on Saturday. Maybe even Friday. Has that changed?"

"No, I'm still thinking about leaving Saturday morning. How about you? When are you planning on leaving?"

"Probably Saturday morning. But it depends on when you leave."

"What do you mean?"

"Well, if you leave tomorrow, I'll probably pack up and go too. We've already found treasure, and with the weekend crowds, I'm not sure I want to be out on the beach alone."

I nodded.

"But if you're staying until Saturday, I'll stay as well. We could spend Friday doing something together."

"Sounds good to me. As long as you don't make me plant more tomatoes or rescue more cars, people, or dogs."

Anna smiled, "I promise there'll be none of that. We'll do something fun."

After we finished our lunch, Anna asked if I'd like to go across the bridge to the mainland to get some supplies for dinner.

"Yeah, sounds good. Who's cooking tonight? Me or you?"

She laughed, "Since your cooking skills seem to be limited to gourmet frozen dinners, I think I better be the cook tonight."

I grinned, "That's what I was hoping you'd say."

As we crossed the bridge to the mainland, Anna pointed to the digital clock on her dash. "It's a little early for dinner. Do you mind if we stop at Target so I can pick up some supplies for my new camper?"

"No problem," I said. "I'm just happy to be along for the ride."

Anna followed Route 60 through Vero to the intersection of Kings highway, and pulled into the Target parking lot.

Inside, she headed for the housewares department where she picked out pillows, pillow cases, sheets, and towels. Then she headed to the kitchen department, where she picked up a silverware set, cooking utensils, plastic glasses, and plates.

Pointing to the cart she said, "This should do." And she headed to the checkout area.

After paying, we headed to the Cruiser and loaded Anna's purchases into the back seat. From Target, we went east on 60 until we reached 21st Street, where we turned left into the Publix grocery store lot.

Inside, Anna picked up a bagged Caesar salad, a hot rotisserie chicken, a key lime pie, and two bottles of white wine.

She looked at me, "Can you think of anything else we need?"

I shook my head, "No, it looks like you've got everything."

Noticing the fully cooked chicken, I asked, "How soon until we eat?"

"As soon as we get back," Anna replied.

Leaving Publix, we headed back onto the island. It took about twenty minutes to get back to the campsite.

When we arrived, I asked, "Will we be eating at your place or mine?"

Anna smiled, "Let's eat at your place. That way Bob won't feel left out. You go ahead and take the food inside. I need to take care of a few things in my camper. I'll be over in a few minutes."

I did as instructed.

Inside the motorhome, Bob was still perched on top of the couch keeping a watchful eye on the birds in the nearby trees.

He looked up at me and said, "Murrfph." He didn't seem too overly excited that I was back.

But when I removed the freshly cooked rotisserie chicken from the shopping bag, it got Bob's attention. He was soon on the floor, purring and rubbing his whiskers against my leg. I was now his best friend in the world.

I said, "Bob, I can see you love me now that I have something you might want to eat."

Bob said, "Murrph."

Anna was at the door a few moments later.

Pointing at the counter, she said, "You take care of the wine. I'll do the rest."

Soon we were at the table eating. Fresh Caesar salad, with roasted chicken breast on the side.

I raised my glass in a toast, "Another hot meal, and not from the microwave. Anna, you're spoiling me."

She smiled mischievously. "You're not spoiled just yet. But it could happen."

I put my hand over my heart, "Anna, you're scaring me."

And I meant it.

67

After dinner, I put the plates in the sink, while Anna cut a chunk of chicken breast into small pieces. After putting the small pieces of chicken on a paper plate, she set it on the floor.

She called out, "Bob. I've got something for you."

I could hear Bob's little feet trotting from the bedroom where he'd been sleeping. He quickly located the plate, cautiously sniffed the morsel of chicken, then looked up at Anna.

"That's right, Bob. It's all for you."

He looked at the plate, and using his front paw reached out and touched the chicken. Withdrawing his paw, he licked it.

That's all it took. Bob hunkered down over the plate and began eating the chicken. Soon after, he began to purr loudly.

Anna turned to me and smiled, "Bob likes roasted chicken."

I nodded, "Yes, and it looks like you're spoiling him, just like you're trying to spoil me!"

Anna smiled. Then she turned serious.

"Remember last night when I said I needed to tell you some things? "

"Yes, I remember."

"Well," she continued, "before I could tell you everything, we were interrupted by Walt. And there's one more thing you need to know. And it may change the way you think about me."

I took a deep breath, "Okay. Tell me."

Anna hesitated, then said, "Remember last Saturday, when I rescued you in the rain storm?"

I nodded, "Of course, how could I forget?"

"Well," she continued, "it wasn't an accident that I found you.

"See, your Sarah had called me. She told me you were going to be camping here, and she asked me to check up on you and Bob."

"Wait a minute," I said, "You know Sarah?"

"Yes, I know Sarah. She and I were roommates when she lived in Bradenton and worked on the charter fishing boat.

"I was working for the power company as a meter reader, and we just hit it off. To save money, we became roomies.

"When the power company transferred me to Vero, I moved out. But she and I have stayed in touch over the years.

"Sarah knew one of my hobbies was metal detecting

and she figured that with the storm coming, I'd probably be heading to Vero Beach.

"So she called and asked me to check up on you and Bob. She wanted to be sure you both were safe."

I shook my head, "If Sarah wanted to know if Bob and I were safe, why didn't she call or text me herself? And why did she want me to come over here in the first place?

"And why when I called, did a guy answer her phone?"

Anna took a sip of her wine.

"Walker, Sarah wanted to tell you this herself, but she was embarrassed. She said I could tell you, as long as I waited until Friday.

"Since it's almost Friday, I guess it will be okay to tell you the full story.

"As you know, Sarah's kayak business wasn't doing too well. With all the new cut-rate competitors coming into town, she wasn't getting many customers.

"She still had bills to pay and was afraid of running out of money. So she started looking for a job. And she didn't want you to know about it."

I interrupted, "What about the lottery money?"

Anna smiled, "The lottery money helped out a lot. She used most of it to pay off her truck and credit card bills. She got out of debt, but didn't have much money left.

"So when she told you she was going into town for

doctor appointments, she was actually going for job interviews.

"Two weeks ago, the yacht club offered her a job as the dock master. And this was exactly what she was hoping for, a chance to work around boats again.

"But there was one little problem. The dock master was a 24/7 job, and they wanted Sarah to move into a small on-site apartment at the club. The apartment would be rent free, and allow her to be close to the dock in case of emergencies.

"Sarah couldn't pass this opportunity up, so she accepted the offer and the job starts Monday.

"She didn't know how to break this to you. Especially the part about her moving and you losing your free camping spot in the boat yard.

"So she figured the best way was to get you out of town while she moved, and then when you got back, she'd break the news to you."

I interrupted. "Anna, if Sarah needed money, she could have asked me. I would have helped her out."

"She said you'd say that. And that's what she was worried about. She was afraid she'd either become dependent on you, or you'd try to talk her out of taking the job.

"Either way, she'd be losing control of her life. And she didn't want that. She didn't want to hurt you either. But she could tell you were getting emotionally attached to her, and that didn't fit in with her plans.

"So she asked me to come over and check on you

and report back to her. And I've been doing just that. I've talked to her several times this week.

"There is some good news though."

"What's that?" I asked.

"Sarah said the rent is paid up on the boatyard for the next eight weeks. So at least you won't need to move right away.

"And there is something else you need to know."

68

"Is it good news or bad?"

Smiling, Anna replied, "I guess it depends on how you feel about Bob.

"See, the reason Sarah wanted you to take Bob this past week is she didn't want him to get hurt or lost during the move to her new apartment.

"And now that she's in the apartment, she has to convince her new boss to allow Bob to live there, because they have a 'no pets' rule.

"So until Sarah can get her boss's approval, she needs you to take care of Bob.

"Will that be a problem?"

I shook my head, "No, no problem. I can take care of Bob for a while. He's pretty easy to live with."

Smiling, Anna said, "Good, I'll let Sarah know. She'll be relieved. And happy that Bob can stay with you."

Bob heard us talking about him, and he came up and nudged Anna. She began stroking his back.

We were both silent while I thought about all she

had just revealed.

My initial reaction was shock and just a twinge of anger. Sarah planned this whole thing, and she and Anna had been talking behind my back all week.

But as I thought it through, I realized there was nothing for me to be angry about. It was a little embarrassing that I was so easy to fool. But all in all, the week had gone well for me. And it had gone well for them, too.

Anna was still petting Bob, when I changed the subject by asking, "So, what are you planning for tomorrow?"

Anna looked up, relief obvious on her face. "So you're not mad at me?"

"No," I replied. "No reason to be. You and I had a good week together, and nothing that you and Sarah did changes that. So everything is cool."

Anna smiled, "Good. That's how I was hoping you'd see it."

She paused, then said, "To answer your question, I'm thinking of going back to Ken's Coins tomorrow and selling the gold ring I found yesterday. You want to come with me?"

I nodded, "Maybe."

She smiled, "Even if you don't want to sell any of your finds, you should bring your coins and get Ken to issue certificates of authenticity for them.

"That'll make them a lot easier to sell later on."

Nodding in agreement, I said, "You're right. I should get them authenticated. Maybe even find out what they're worth while I'm there."

Anna stood, "I plan to leave around nine in the morning. Be ready then." She turned and headed for the door.

"Wait," I said, "where are you going? It's still early. I figured we'd hang out here for a while. Maybe talk a bit more about what's happened this week."

Sarah shook her head, "No can do. I've got some things I need to take care of over in my camper."

She turned, gave me a kiss on the cheek and said, "See you in the morning." Then she walked out the door.

I looked at Bob. "Well buddy, it looks like it's going to be just you and me tonight."

69

The next morning Bob woke me at dawn. The birds had returned to the tree outside his window, and he wanted me to be aware of the possibilities they presented.

When he jumped up on the bed, then sat on my chest, I ignored him, hoping he'd go away. But he didn't. Instead, he reached out with his paw and tapped me on the cheek.

"Okay Bob. You win. I'll get up."

Bob said, "Murrph," then jumped down from the bed and ran into the bathroom to inspect his food.

Seeing that his bowl was still full from the night before, he strutted to the couch, jumped up on the back and found a comfortable spot where he could lay against the screen and spy on the birds outside.

His small bump of a tail twitched and he made a clicking sound in his throat as small birds jumped from limb to limb just out of his reach.

Bob was happy.

Me? I would have rather slept in for another hour.

But now that I was awake, I pulled on my shoes, ran a hand through my hair, grabbed my keys, and headed out for an early morning walk.

As I had done the first day at the park, I headed east toward the Sebastian Inlet fishing pier, a brisk ten minute walk from my campsite.

Upon reaching the pier, I could see that even at this early hour, there were several people with fishing poles extended out over the pier's railing, hoping to catch a big one with the incoming tide.

As I passed one of the men at the rail, he turned and said, "Hey, it's Mr. Lucky. Stop and talk for a minute."

It was the same fisherman I had talked to six days earlier.

I smiled. "Good morning. How's the fishing?"

The man nodded at the three fishing rods he was tending, "Not so good. Water's still stirred up from the storm. But at least the weather's a lot better today than it was the last time I saw you."

"You're right about that."

I nodded toward one of his rods, "Looks like you might have something on that line."

He turned and saw that the line was twitching and the rod bent toward the water.

Smiling, he said, "Yep, you're still my good luck charm." He then picked up the rod and started reeling in his catch.

I waved and walked off. Time to head back to the motorhome.

After a quick shower, I had a breakfast of cold cereal. Then I emptied the remaining cereal into the trash, and set the empty box on the dinette table.

Back in the bedroom, I lifted the bed platform, and unlocked the storage compartment under the bed.

Gathering up the gold and silver coins and the ring, I took them up front and laid them out on the dinette table. There I carefully placed each item, wrapped in a paper towel, into the empty cereal box.

I figured carrying my treasures in a cereal box was a lot safer than carrying them in a money bag while out in public.

Around nine, Anna knocked on the door.

"Walker, you up?"

I opened the door, "Yep, I'm up and ready to go."

She pointed to the cereal box I was holding. "You plan to eat in the car?"

"No. I've got my coins in the box."

She nodded, "Not a bad idea. But walking around carrying a cereal box? You can do better than that."

She walked to the kitchen counter and picked up one of the empty Publix grocery bags from our shopping trip the day before.

Handing me the bag, she said, "Put the box in this. It won't look so strange that way."

She was right. Walking around with a grocery bag

wouldn't attract nearly as much attention as walking around holding a box of cereal. I did as she suggested, and we headed out.

It took us about twenty five minutes to get to Ken's coin shop. And as before, the door was locked when we arrived.

Anna pressed the buzzer, and a moment later we heard Ken's voice on the intercom.

"Anna, did you bring me some more goodies?"

"Maybe. Buzz us in and find out."

The door buzzed and we heard the bolt unlock.

Before entering, Anna looked around to make sure no one was behind us. Satisfied we weren't be followed, we went in.

Inside, Ken was waiting for us sitting on the stool on his side of the counter.

"So, what did you bring me today?", he asked.

Anna reached into her pocket and pulled out the ring she'd found two days earlier.

Ken looked at the ring and said, "Nice. Looks to be old gold."

He weighed it on a nearby scale. "A little over fourteen grams. Melt value is around a thousand. You find this on the beach?"

Anna nodded, "Yes."

"So it's probably from the 1715 fleet?"

Anna nodded again, "I think so."

Ken paused, then said, "I'll give you three thousand for it."

Anna shook her head. "No way. A gold ring from the 1715 fleet is worth a lot more than that."

Ken smiled, "Just testing you. Fifty five hundred. Cash today."

Anna smiled, "Agreed."

Ken took the ring and put it below the counter. He then went to the back office and returned a few moments later with fifty five one hundred dollar bills.

He handed them to Anna, and asked, "Got anything else?"

Anna looked at me, and pointed to the plastic bag that held my cereal box.

"Walker here has a few things."

Ken looked my way, "Okay, let's see what you have."

I reached into the box and took out the first clump of silver coins and placed them on the rubber mat on the counter.

Pointing at the coins, Ken asked, "May I?"

I nodded, giving Ken permission to examine them.

He picked up the clump. "Not bad. A cluster of four reale coins. Looks to be about forty in this clump. A nice artifact. Worth a few thousand dollars."

Putting the clump back on the counter, Ken asked, "What else you got?"

I pulled out the second clump of coins and placed them on the mat.

Ken nodded, "Nice. A larger clump. More coins. Probably seventy in this clump. Worth some money for sure."

"What else?"

I reached back into the box and retrieved the three gold coins and placed them on the mat.

Ken inspected each coin, then asked, "Are these from the same place the coins Anna had the other day?"

I nodded, "Yep, they sure are."

Ken looked at the collection of treasure I'd placed before him. "Nice haul. You did good. Anything else?"

I shook my head, "That's it for now."

He picked up his calculator and started entering numbers.

Before he could give me a total, Anna's phone rang. She answered it immediately.

"This is Anna... Yes, I told him."

"Hold on a minute."

Putting the phone up against her chest, Anna turned to me and said, "I need to take this call. I'll be outside. You take as long as you want in here. This might be a long call."

Turning to Ken, she smiled and said, "As always, a pleasure dealing with you. Buzz me out will you?"

After she'd left, Ken looked up at me, "Shall we continue?"

I nodded.

"On the gold coins, I can give you the same as I gave Anna. Seven thousand each.

"On the clusters of silver coins, I'll give you four thousand for the smaller one, and seven thousand for the larger. All together it comes in at thirty two thousand dollars."

Nodding, I said, "The prices seem fair, but I want to keep one of the gold coins."

"Okay, but that brings the total down to twenty five thousand."

I nodded, "Sounds good to me. Let's do it."

Ken walked to his back office, and returned with documents for me to sign and a red bank bag.

After I signed, he opened the bank bag and handed me five stacks of hundred dollar bills, each marked 'five thousand.'

"Count it", he said.

After I counted the money, I nodded to Ken, "It's all here. Thanks."

Gathering up everything except the one gold coin I was keeping, Ken asked, "You want me to issue a certificate of authenticity for this?"

"Yes, that'd be good."

Reaching under the counter, he retrieved a pre-printed form. Picking up a pen, he wrote some notes about the coin I was keeping. Then he signed the form, and using a hand stamp, notarized it with his seal.

Sliding the form across the counter to me, he said, "Keep this with the coin. It'll make it easier to sell."

Then he asked, "Anything else?"

Pausing for a moment, I decided to see what the gold ring with the emerald in it might be worth. I reached into the box, pulled it out and set it on the rubber mat in front of Ken.

Carefully unwrapping the paper towel from around the ring, I placed it on the mat in front of Ken so the emerald was facing up at him.

Upon seeing the ring, he took a deep breath.

"Is that what I think it is?" he asked.

70

"I don't know," I replied. "What do you think it is?"

Ken picked up his jeweler's loupe and examined the ring. He said nothing as he was doing this.

Then he put the ring down and said, "You really don't know what this is?"

I shook my head, "No. Tell me."

"See the marking on the side? That's King Felipe of Spain's family crest. The initials on the other side would be those of a ship's captain.

"This is a King's Authority ring and it gives the wearer the power to act at as an agent of the King.

"The wearer can seize land, make treaties, assign right, and assert the authority of the King in trade matters.

"These rings were only given to the King's most trusted confidants. Sometimes, ship captains and new world explorers would get them. But they are very rare.

"Only two other King Felipe authority rings are known to still exist. One is in the Vatican, and the other is in Mel Fisher's treasure vault."

Ken paused, then looked at me, "You want to sell it?"

"Maybe. Tell me what it's worth."

Reaching into his pocket, Ken removed his phone. "Mind if I shoot a few photo of it? I've got someone who can give me a better idea of the price once they see it."

"Go ahead," I said. "Take as many photos as you want. As long as I'm not in them."

Ken shot three photos of the ring, and sent them to someone on his phone's contact list.

A few moments later his phone rang. I could only hear one side of the conversation.

"Yeah, this is Ken... Yes, I've got the ring right here."

"Yeah, I think it is real."

A pause, then, "Yeah, it was found on the beach this week. No one else has seen it... Okay. Hold on."

Ken put the phone down and said, "My buyer says seventy five thousand. Cash. Today."

I smiled. "That's a lot of money. But I think I'll pass."

Ken shook his head, then picked up the phone.

"The seller said no. He's going to keep it."

Then into the phone, "Are you sure?"

Ken put the phone down and looked at me. "One hundred and fifty thousand."

I smiled, "That's getting closer. But still not there

yet."

Ken groaned, then told the buyer, "No. Not enough."

Then, "Okay, I'll tell him."

Ken put the phone down again, "The buyer says he'll do two hundred fifty thousand, and can have a cashier's check in your hands in ten minutes. But that's his final offer."

I smiled, "Sounds good. Let's do it."

Ken returned to the phone, "It's a deal."

Then, "Okay, I'll tell him. We'll get it signed. Ten minutes. Sounds good."

Ken ended the call, then turned to me. "The buyer is sending a cashier's check. It'll be drawn on SunTrust bank. There's a branch office in this shopping center. You can take the check over there to make sure it's good."

I nodded.

"The buyer wants you to sign a non-disclosure agreement promising to never reveal to anyone what you sold the ring for, or to who.

"You won't be able to tell anyone, not even Anna, about what you got for the ring, or what kind of ring it is. Any problem with that?"

I shook my head. "No, that's fine."

"Good, wait right here."

Ken went to his back office and returned a moment later holding three sheets of paper. He put these, along with a pen, on the counter in front of me.

"The first is the non-disclosure. The second is a statement saying you found the ring on the beach, and not in the water, that makes it a legal find. And the third is a statement saying you are giving up all claims to the ring."

I looked at each document, then signed them.

As I was handing the papers back to Ken, his door buzzer sounded. Ken pointed at the security monitor behind the counter, which showed a man in a suit standing outside at the door, a manila folder tucked under his arm.

Ken buzzed him in.

The man came in and handed Ken the folder. Ken inspected the contents, thanked the man, and buzzed him back out.

Returning his attention to me, Ken said, "This is your check. You can see that it is made out to the bearer and is in the amount of two hundred fifty thousand dollars.

Looking up at me, he asked, "Do you have an account at SunTrust?"

I nodded, "Sure do."

"Good. If you'd like, I can call the branch manager and let him know you're coming over. He'll verify the check, and then deposit it into your account."

I nodded, "Do that. Tell him I'll be right over."

Ken picked up his phone and made the call.

"It's all set. He'll be waiting for you."

I thanked Ken, and he buzzed me out. He had given me a plain brown paper bag to hold the cash he'd paid me, along with the cashier's check and the gold coin I was keeping.

Outside, Anna was sitting in the Cruiser, still on the phone.

I signaled to her that I was going to walk to the end of the shopping center, and she nodded 'okay.'

Five minutes later I was sitting in the bank manager's office. I'd given him the check and my bank account number.

He punched a few keys on his computer, and a moment later, a teller walked into his office and handed him a deposit receipt showing that two hundred fifty thousand had been deposited into my account.

Handing me the receipt, the manager said, "The money is now in your account. You can draw on it immediately."

I took the receipt, checked it, and smiled. The money was there.

The manager rechecked his computer screen, then turned toward me with a smile and said, "Mr. Walker, I see you have a very large balance in your checking account. Would you like to speak to one of our investment advisers?"

I shook my head, "No thanks. Not today."

Leaving the bank with the deposit slip safely tucked

away, and the paper bag from Ken under my arm, I headed back toward Anna and her Land Cruiser. She saw me coming and quickly ended her phone call.

As soon as I opened the passenger door and climbed in, she asked, "How'd it go with Ken? He treat you right?"

I smiled, "It went well. He seems to be a good guy."

She nodded, then said, "That was Sarah on the phone."

"That's what I figured. How's she doing?"

"Pretty good. She's excited about her new job and her new apartment.

"She wanted to know if I'd told you yet. And how you took it."

I nodded, "What'd you tell her?"

"I told her you were happy that she landed her dream job."

"I also told her not to worry about you. You were a big boy and could take care of yourself."

I laughed. She was right.

We spent the rest of the day playing tourists. We visited the Mel Fisher Treasure Museum, walked the docks at the marina, ate lunch at Captain Hiram's on the Riverfront, visited a few specialty shops, and ended our day back at Publix, where we picked up supplies for our final dinner together.

Back at the campground, Anna prepared dinner in

the Love Bus. I tried to help, but she said, "You open the wine, I'll do the rest."

After dinner, she suggested we go outside, sit at the picnic table, finish our wine and watch the sun go down.

We were starting on our second glass when Anna reached over and took my hand. "There's something I need to tell you."

"Again? You're full of secrets aren't you?

"Is this one going to be good or bad?"

She smiled, "I think it's going to be good."

She paused, then announced, "We're going to be roommates."

"Roommates? You and Sarah?"

"No, silly. You and me. We're going to be roommates. At least for a while."

"See, about two weeks ago I mentioned to Sarah that I was planning on moving back to Englewood.

"Then a week later, she called and told me about her new job and the apartment she was moving into. During that call, she said that since the rent was paid up on her old apartment, I could live there while I looked for another place.

"But there was a catch. She said there was this guy living in a motorhome in her back yard. And I wasn't too sure about that. About a strange guy living in the back yard.

"But as it turns out, you're the guy. And now that I

305

know you, it seems like a good idea. So we're going to be roommates. You and me."

I shook my head, "So let me get this straight. You're moving to Englewood, and will be living in Sarah's old apartment?"

"That's right. Except, her old apartment doesn't have any furniture in it, so I'll just pull my camper up next to yours, and live in it.

"Won't that be great!"

I shook my head, "I'm not sure what it will be. But what about work? What will you do to make a living?"

Anna smiled, "That won't be a problem. While on medical leave after the attack, I studied and got my Florida real estate license.

"I've been offered a job with a local real estate office in Englewood.

"So when we both get back over there, I can be your real estate agent. I can help you find the perfect place."

I stopped her, "Anna, it sounds like you've got this all figured out. Except for one thing. What makes you think I'm going to be buying a place?"

She smiled and patted my hand, "Walker, you'll see. You can't live in other people's backyards forever. You're going to want your own place."

I nodded, "That may be so, but why would I want you as a real estate agent?"

Anna smiled, "You're going to want me as your agent because when I worked for the power company as a meter reader, I visited every home in the Englewood area at least once a month.

"I can tell you which neighborhoods are good and which are bad. I can tell you which areas flood and which are always high and dry.

"And I know hidden away places that most other agents won't know about.

"And that's why you'll want me as your real estate agent. Because I can find the right place for you."

Then she held up her wine glass, "Let's toast, roomie!"

I just shook my head.

I guess it was settled. I'd just lost my old roommate, and gained a new one.

And little did I know that a new, bigger adventure was just beginning.

The adventure continues . . .

Follow the adventures of Walker and Mango Bob in the Mango Bob series of books found at Amazon.

Find photos, maps, and more from the Mango Bob adventures at http://www.mangobob.com

Facebook: www.facebook.com/MangoBob

If you liked *Mango Lucky*, please post a review at Amazon, and let your friends know about the Mango Bob series.

Other books by Bill Myers:

Mango Bob

Buying a used motorhome without getting burned

Metal Detecting Florida Beaches

29715499R00192

Made in the USA
San Bernardino, CA
29 January 2016